MURDER ON POINTE

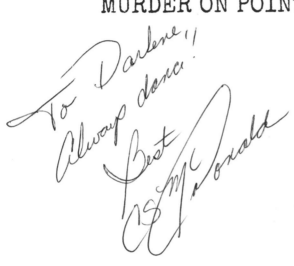

To Darlene,!
Always dance!
Best
CS McDonald

MURDER ON POINTE

A Fiona Quinn Mystery

C.S. McDonald

ISBN-13: 9780991368075
ISBN-10: 099136807X
Library of Congress Control Number: 2016911114
McWriter Books, Hookstown, PA

For my beautiful granddaughters, Kiersten, Riley, and Abigail. I love you with all my heart.

Acknowledgements

Beta reader one: Linda Taylor
Beta reader two: Lauren Carr
Editor: Sherri Good, Silver Lining Editing Services
Proofreader: Renee Waring, Guardian Proofreading Services
Cover design: Dawne Dominique, DusktilDawn Designs

I would like to thank all of these wonderful people listed above for their hard work to make this book possible.

One

Fiona Quinn whipped her blue and white Mini Cooper into the tight corner parking space that no SUV or full-size sedans would dare attempt. Her lips curled into a smile because she had scored a spot on the second level of the parking garage a little more than a block from the Benedum Center located in downtown Pittsburgh.

Thirty minutes ahead of schedule, she lay her head back against the rest to listen to the overture from the classic ballet, Coppelia, filtering from the CD player. It was her favorite ballet, and she had been waiting, not so patiently, for months to see it.

Coppelia was the enchanting story of an old inventor named Dr. Coppelius who created beautiful, life-like dolls in his shop. His most elegant creation was a doll named Coppelia and he adored her so. Each day, he'd display his exquisite invention on the balcony of his shop, intriguing all the townspeople. They would try and try to get Coppelia's attention, to no avail. The girl would simply sit on the balcony, supposedly reading her book, ignoring everyone. Like the townsfolk, Franz, who is engaged to Swanhilda, believes she is a real girl. He falls helplessly in love with the mysterious maiden. Swanhilda becomes enraged and sets out to prove that Coppelia is nothing more than a fake.

To add to the excitement of attending her all-time favorite ballet, her old friend, Silja (Sil-ya) Ramsay, was dancing the principal role, Swanhilda. Coppelia had been the last ballet Silja performed in before returning to the US from Russia, where she was the principal dancer for the Novikov Ballet Company. Fiona couldn't wait to watch her dance.

Ahhh, the music seduced her into wonderful memories of standing at the barre in front of the huge mirrors beside Silja working tendus, ron de jambs, and grand battements at the Pittsburgh Ballet Theater School where they'd studied as teens. She remembered the Ballet Mistress calling out, "Legs straight! Chin up! Shoulders back! Fiona, tuck your tush!"

Silja went on to become a professional dancer.

Fiona—a kindergarten teacher.

No, teaching was not nearly as glamorous a career as wearing sparkling tutus and tiaras or taking curtain calls while audience members throw roses onto the stage. However Fiona was happy working with children, and that's what mattered.

As the overture finished and the CD swept on to track one, Fiona turned her cell phone off. She gathered up her black clutch from the passenger's seat and reluctantly got out of her warm car to face the bitter chill February would blast at her during the block or so walk.

As she approached the elevator a tall handsome man swept past her. Not so much as glancing in her direction, he hurried through the garage while raking his fingers through his dark hair. They met again at the elevator along with an old woman leaning on a wooden cane, wrapped up like a mummy with a red wool scarf over her head, and a dark wool coat that was a size or so too big for her. She was trying to press the buttons for the elevator. The man stood next to her, tugging at his coat, biting his lip, and tapping his foot.

The woman smiled at Fiona through wrinkled lips. "My old fingers just don't want to work in this terrible cold." She rubbed her gloved hands together as if they pained her.

"Here, let me help," Fiona offered, except the man reached in front of her to quickly stab the button with his finger. Both women glanced at him. Avoiding their gaze, he shifted from one foot to the other waiting for the elevator to arrive.

"Don't you look pretty?" the old woman said. "Are you going to the ballet?" The elevator doors opened. The man hurried aboard. The old woman hobbled into the car, Fiona following. Still the man shifted his weight around. Fiona and the woman watched him, trying to figure out if he was cold, late for an appointment, or perhaps both.

Deciding to ignore him, Fiona answered the woman's question. "I am. I have an old friend dancing the role of Swanhilda today. We're having lunch afterward. I can't wait to see her."

"You must be talking about our guest dancer, Silja Ramsay. I've watched her rehearse. She's absolutely wonderful."

"Do you work at the Benedum?" Fiona inquired.

The bell dinged and the doors slid open. The man leapt from the car and hurried away. Leaning heavily on her cane, the old woman shuffled out. "Yes, I do. Enjoy the performance and your lunch."

"Would you like me to walk with you?"

"Oh, no, my dear. I'm much too slow. Be on your way. There's no use both of us slowly freezing to death." The woman smiled again, urging her forward with a sweep of her cane.

Fiona studied the old lady's face. Through the lines and creases there was evidence of a once attractive woman. She favored her with a parting smile and then hunkered into her big fur collar to face the bluster. With long quick strides she arrived at the tall glass doors of the theater. She checked her chin length strawberry blonde hair and red lipstick in the reflection before presenting her ticket to the usher just inside the door. Unbuttoning her coat, she stepped into the exquisite red carpeted lobby flanked by ornate curved staircases. Vendors were selling T-shirts, detailed program books, and other Coppelia paraphernalia. Little girls pointed and begged at the autographed worn pointe shoes also for sale. Fiona smiled. She remembered her mother buying her a pair when she was just five. Breathing in deep, she took in the inviting aroma of roasted almonds wafting through the din of theater goers, as she passed the wine bar and the line of people waiting to buy a long pointy bag of the warmed almond treats.

She found her seat in the third row behind the orchestra—dead center, and as she perused her program looking for Silja's bio, she noticed another name among the cast that she recognized. She smiled at the thought of her old Ballet Master, David Sheppard, playing the role of Dr. Coppelius. Very apropos, in her opinion. She figured that he must be at least sixty-five years old by now, and that made her wonder about the old woman she'd met in the parking garage. She looked to be about the same age. She said that she worked at the Benedum. While she couldn't see what the woman was wearing because of her heavy coat, Fiona didn't imagine that she was an usher. If she was, she was quite late for work.

The thought of the old woman and the parking garage reminded her that Silja had requested that Fiona meet her at the stage door twenty minutes after the performance ended so they would have plenty of time to lunch. Silja needed to get back to the theater in ample time to prepare for the eight o'clock performance. There was no parking in that area, and no, you were not permitted to simply pull up to the curb and wait for someone, but people did it all the time.

Fiona sighed and hoped a police officer wouldn't come along and give her a ticket for sitting along the curb. It would be bad enough that angry drivers would honk their horns, demanding that she move her car. She rolled her eyes at the thought. Hopefully, Silja would be timely. She couldn't think about it now, she wanted to enjoy the ballet. She'd worry it out when the time came. *Yeah, sure.* She had no doubt her subconscious would be fretting about it through the entire performance.

Ugh.

At last, the theater's huge sparkling crystal Austrian chandelier dimmed until it darkened completely. The audience hushed. The orchestra played the same overture she'd listened to in the car, only the live music filled her soul with joy. It was time to forget the meeting arrangements and just relax. Finally the curtains swept open for the Saturday afternoon performance of Coppelia.

—~m~—

Holding her breath, Fiona eased her car up to the curb near the stage door, as she feared, the honking began the instant she pulled to the curb. She was thankful Silja was waiting on the stoop huddled in her long furry coat. Her golden brunette hair was pulled back in a severe bun. Her nose, cheeks, and ears were rosy. Just as she started down the three steps to the sidewalk a slender red-headed woman pushed through the door into the afternoon chill.

Opening the car door, Silja called to the young woman, "Have a nice afternoon, Monroe."

Glaring, the tall thin redhead snapped, "That's not going to happen anytime soon."

"I'm sorry to hear that."

"I'll just bet you are."

Uncomfortable with the exchange between her friend and the woman and the horns honking all around her, Fiona fidgeted in her seat. After what seemed like forever, Silja slipped into the passenger's seat of the Mini Cooper and slammed the door, but before Fiona could pull forward into traffic, a sleek silver Mercedes pulled to the curb blocking her movement. Monroe took her time getting to the vehicle, and then just as she was about to ease into the passenger's seat, she slammed the door to hurry back inside the theater.

"Who is that?" Fiona asked.

"Oh, that's Monroe McCarthy. I think it's a stage name," Silja scoffed, rolling her eyes. Fiona chuckled. "Anyway, she's a soloist who was first in line for the position of principal dancer after Julianna Fields decided to leave PBT to get married and have babies. But for some reason, they by-passed her and invited me to dance the role of Swanhilda while their other principal dancer, Alexis Cartwright, dances the role of Swanhilda's friend. Monroe plays the role of Coppelia, who is on the stage most of the ballet, but there really isn't as much dancing. She's mad because they brought me in. I think she believes I'm permanent, but I've got a husband and my own dance school to get home to when the show closes in a few weeks."

"Why don't you just tell her that? Maybe she'd settle down and be a little nicer to you." The Mercedes pulled forward against the curb, allowing Fiona to volley for position in traffic among the irritated drivers. After several rude gestures were flung in her direction, she wasn't sure if she was grateful to the driver of the Mercedes or not.

Silja shrugged. "The Ballet Mistress wants to let her stew. I'm not exactly sure why. It's none of my business. She'll either get the position when I leave or she won't."

"She seems like a vindictive person. Monroe, I mean, and maybe the Ballet Mistress too."

Quick movement from the Mercedes caught Fiona's attention. A man in a dark coat and a plaid muffler got out of the car to rush toward the open stage door. She couldn't see who he was calling to, nor did she have a clear view of the man. A horn honked loud and long, urging her forward, bringing her attention back to the traffic now on the move.

Silja was still in the midst of explaining, "Oh, what you saw was nothing. When I left the dressing room she was having it out with Alexis."

"What about?"

"From what I gather, Monroe's parents are coming to the ballet tomorrow and I guess she wants to dance a bigger part. Alexis told her no. Monroe went into a total tantrum, yelling and screaming and calling her names. I don't know why she would even bother Alexis about trading positions. You're not allowed to just switch roles around because you want to. That all has to be approved by PBT. She's a real piece of work, that one."

Fiona winced. "Sounds like it."

"Hey, let's forget about her. We haven't seen each other in such a long time. I want to catch up, not talk about someone who won't be a part of my life two weeks from now." She kissed Fiona on the cheek. "So, how've ya been, Sugar Twin?"

Fiona chuckled at the usual Silja antics. "I've been just fine. So, three weeks of rehearsal and two weeks of performances, doesn't your husband mind you being away so long?"

"Grant works out of town a lot."

"That works, I guess. What does he do? Sales?"

Silja shifted in her seat. "Let's just say he's a man on a mission."

Strange answer. Fiona maneuvered the Cooper along busy Penn Avenue toward the Fort Pitt Bridge. "You danced beautifully today, Silja. I was so proud of you."

"Thanks. I wish you were still dancing, Fiona. It would be so much fun to work together. It's too bad what happened. Does your knee still give you trouble?"

Fiona sighed at the memory of the skiing accident when she was nineteen. She'd ripped her meniscus so badly that it required surgery. The recovery took forever and the doctor didn't feel that a career in dance would be the best option, so Fiona's parents convinced her to attend Clarion University for a teaching degree.

"It's been almost ten years, but yes, it still pinches from time to time. My dancing days are long gone, except for the Zumba classes that I take on Thursday evenings. Not exactly the same thing, but they're fun."

—◊◊◊—

The lunch at Vincent's in nearby Greentree had been quick. Fiona wished they had more time to spend together. When they returned to the city at six-forty-five, Silja insisted that Fiona accompany her to the dressing room. "C'mon," she cajoled, "It'll be fun. You haven't been in the backstage area of the Benedum since we danced in the Nutcracker when we were nineteen."

"Oh yeah, that was the ballet before my tumble down the slopes at Seven Springs," Fiona recalled.

Silja winced apologetically. "Sorry, bad memory. Won't you come anyway? This way we'll have a little more time together." She laid her head on her old friend's shoulder while batting her eyelashes in an attempt to persuade her. *Yep, Silja and her antics—still at it after all these years.*

Fiona chuckled. "Oh, why not? Okay, it'll be fun to see the dressing rooms again after so long."

After parking the Mini Cooper in the garage, the girls hurried along the street toward the Benedum while giggling and joking about some of the Ballet Mistresses they'd dealt with as teens.

"Do you remember Gisela?" Fiona asked.

"Who could forget Mistress Gisela?" Silja laughed. "Her German accent bounced off the studio walls. I swear, I never understood one word the woman said."

"Oh! Do you remember the day she walked right up to Amber Archer at the barre and screamed into her face, *your mother is wasting her money?*"

Silja laid her hand over her chest. "Oh yes, it was awful. Now I understood *that* quite clearly. But in her defense, Amber wasn't the most motivated dancer in the class. As I recall, she was a bit too chubby to be at PBT too."

"Maybe. She could've lost about fifteen to twenty pounds, I suppose," Fiona said. "I wonder whatever happened to Amber. She didn't return to PBT the next year."

"I remember hearing a rumor that she spiked Mistress Gisela's water bottle with a huge dose of Milk of Magnesia. Not good. I heard she was kicked out—but it was a rumor."

"I certainly hope so," Fiona said.

"Maybe she just moved away. Who knows? She probably became a *kindergarten* teacher."

"It happens," Fiona snorted and stepped into the crosswalk. A man, coming from the opposite curb, plowed right into Fiona. She fell backward to the pavement.

"Fiona!" Silja cried out, as she grabbed her hand to pull her to her feet. "Are you okay?"

Dazed, Fiona brushed the snow and street crud from her coat. "I think so…"

They both looked toward the sidewalk. The man had kept right on walking—practically jogging. "Do you believe that?" Silja said in disgust. "He didn't even stop to see if you were okay or to help you up. I guess chivalry really is dead."

Fiona stared at the man. She'd seen him some-where before. A horn honked, insisting that they get out of the way, jerking her attention back to where they stood.

"C'mon, the light turned green. We'd better get to the curb before they run us over," Silja said, as she pulled Fiona toward the sidewalk. Fiona limped a little until she loosened up again during the half-block walk. "Are you sure you're okay?" Silja asked.

They scurried through the stage door entrance to escape the bitter cold that was getting worse by the moment. The skies turned a dark ashen as a snow flurry began.

"I'm fine," Fiona insisted.

"Whatta jerk that guy was."

"Mmmm."

Fiona felt strange being in the backstage area of the theater after such a long absence. The halls were dimly lit and quiet. It was an eerie place where dancers, singers, and actors from years past roamed the halls waiting for their stage calls. Even as a young girl she could feel them lurking there, waiting, anticipating their cue to walk out into the spotlight. The Benedum was once known as the Stanley Theater, but they didn't care. It was their theater, and so they remained—waiting, anticipating.

"Hi, Sara," Fiona heard Silja say.

A young dancer hurrying down the hall turned. "Oh…hi. I thought I was the only one here. Got to get my makeup going. See you backstage," she said just before disappearing around the corner.

Fiona cocked her head to one side. The dancer looked familiar. Her brunette hair with cinnamon strands accentuated her pixie green eyes, except how would she know her? Unless perhaps she'd seen her at the Robinson Mall or at the strip district, shopping.

"Sara Holloway, such a hard-working dancer. Always arrives before everyone else to warm up."

"She looks so familiar. Where is she from?"

"Alexis said she came in from Philadelphia about six months ago. She's a real sweetheart."

"I don't remember seeing her name in the program," Fiona said.

"She didn't dance the matinee today. Don't know why." Silja pulled the silver pashmina scarf from around her neck as she opened the dressing room door only to come to an abrupt halt. Her body tensed, while she gasped at something inside the room.

"What is it, Silja? What's wrong?"

Hesitantly, Silja stepped through the door. She whispered, "Alexis…" but the blonde ballerina didn't respond. Her upper body lay slumped over the surface of the lighted vanity, motionless. While Fiona peered over her shoulder, Silja approached her friend with slow deliberate steps. "Alexis…are you all right?"

Fiona squeezed Silja's shoulder. "You don't thinks she's…"

Trembling, Silja reached down to lay her fingers gently on the dancer's neck and then quickly jerked her hand away to clutch the front of her coat. "I don't believe it. She's…she's dead." Silja looked around the room.

Noticing blood splatter on the mirror above the vanity, on an empty vase that probably once held flowers from an adoring fan, and other small items knocked about the vanity top, Fiona stepped past her friend to the other side of the vanity. She gasped. "There's blood coming from her head on this side. Someone hit her over the head. Who would do such a thing?"

"I hope that I don't know."

"Silja, we can't wait, we need to call 9-1-1, immediately."

"Absolutely. Be careful not to touch anything in the room," Silja instructed.

"Well, of course not, we don't want to contaminate a crime scene—I watch TV."

The girls hurried from the room, and just as Fiona eased the door closed behind them, Monroe slipped into the dressing room one door down. The girls exchanged wary glances, as Silja pulled her phone from her purse and dialed 9-1-1.

Two

Within fifteen minutes the Benedum Center was surrounded by flashing lights. Police officers poured into the theater, while a crowd of frustrated ticket holders gathered at the curb along with Pittsburghers who were just wondering what was going on. News crews arrived, vying for any and all information they could glean about the dead body discovered inside the grand old theater.

As instructed by first responders, Fiona and Silja waited in the hallway outside the dressing room to give a statement to a police detective. Trying to stay out of the way, Silja clung to Fiona's hand, while they watched a police officer stretch yellow crime scene tape across the doorway. Flashes from a camera illuminated the room like a strobe light.

A shiver ran down Fiona's spine. How awful to be photographed in death after being beaten about the head. She glanced at Silja, who watched the scene play out with quiet trepidation washing over her face and stance.

"Are you okay, Ms. Ramsay?" a man asked in a soft tone.

The girls turned to find an older gentleman with grey curls and a gentle smile standing nearby.

Silja said, "As good as can be expected. Thanks, Calvin."

He let out a beleaguered sigh. "I feel so bad. Ms. Cartwright was a nice girl."

"She truly was. We're waiting for the detective to talk with us."

"I'm collecting up my maintenance crew. They want us all to go to the theater. If there's anything I can get you, don't be afraid to ask."

The sound of a door clicking closed made them turn. The old woman that Fiona had met in the garage stepped out of a room two doors down from the murder scene. Tugging her red scarf around her shoulders, she shuffled down the hallway, holding onto the wall. Calvin hurried to catch up.

Touching her lightly on the shoulder he said, "Please go to the theater and have a seat with the rest of the crew. I'll walk along with you. How's your headache?"

"Not much better, I'm afraid," the woman said.

"I can get you some Ibuprofen or an aspirin."

"Thank you, Calvin." The old woman glanced back to see Fiona, hesitated, tossed her a guarded smile, and then continued down the hallway.

How strange. Turning to Silja, she asked, "Who was that man?"

"That was Calvin Kleppner. He's been the head of the maintenance crew here at Benedum for years. Such a sweet man. I'm surprised you don't remember him."

She shook her head. "I don't."

Just then several men arrived wearing surly expressions, latex gloves, and carrying silver boxes. They ducked under the tape to enter the dressing room. Hushed conversations filtered into the hallway, but Fiona couldn't make out what was being said.

Leaning in close, she whispered to Silja. "Looks like the murder police are here."

"You mean the crime scene investigators?"

"No, I think she means me," a man said. The girls snapped their heads up to find an attractive thirty-ish man standing in front of them. With his eyes fixed on Calvin and the old woman making their way down the hallway, he popped a bite size chocolate bar into his mouth. Around the candy he said, "I'm Detective Nathan Landry, homicide division of the Pittsburgh Police Department." The pair turned the corner. The detective returned his gaze to the girls. "I understand that you ladies discovered Ms. Cartwright's body."

Fiona found Detective Landry's voice soothing. It had a calm, take charge tone about it without sounding demanding or accusing. His dark hair swept just above his deep brown eyes—the color of coffee. He had dimples. She'd never thought of a homicide detective having dimples. Although Tom Selleck has dimples, but he's an actor who plays a detective, he's not a real detective. How silly.

He shook Silja's hand. "Silja Ramsay," she supplied.

When he shook Fiona's hand, she was impressed with his firm yet welcoming grip—not to mention he wasn't wearing a wedding ring. He glanced down at his notepad. "And you're Fiona Quinn—not a member of the cast. What you were doing in the dressing room, Ms. Quinn?"

"I'm an old friend of Silja's."

"I see, so you didn't know Ms. Cartwright?"

He was looking right into her eyes. Detective Landry wasn't quite as handsome as Tom Selleck. The detective was more attractive than ruggedly handsome as the older yet yummy actor was. Still, she was having a little trouble concentrating on his questions. "What? Oh, no…no, I've never met Ms. Cartwright before today. I mean I've never met her at all. I guess I never will actually meet her, since she's been murdered and all. Even though I don't know her, I feel really bad for what happened to her. I'm sure she didn't deserve it. I mean, nobody *deserves* to be murdered—" She let out a frustrated breath. "I just came to spend time with Silja, and then all this—"

He nodded his understanding, and then he cocked his head to one side. "Yinz didn't touch anything in the room, right?"

"Only Alexis," Silja said.

"Why did you touch her?"

"I was checking for a pulse."

"Because you thought she was dead?"

"I was afraid that she was, yes."

"Why did you think she was dead?"

Fiona could see that Silja was taken aback by his line of questioning. Her jaw worked, but nothing came out for a few seconds. Finally she curtly replied, "Because she was slumped in her chair, I suppose."

"Ms. Cartwright never slumped?"

"Well, no…I-I don't think so anyway."

He smiled. Relief washed through her, easing her worry that he was about to accuse them of killing Alexis.

"In any case, your assumption was correct. Ms. Cartwright is in fact dead."

Snarky, Detective Landry is snarky. She kind of liked that about him. She didn't believe that Tom Selleck was ever snarky. One point for the cute detective.

He went on to ask all the usual detective murder questions like, did Alexis have any enemies in the cast or did Silja know of anyone who would want to do her harm? Was there a boyfriend in the picture, and if so was he a nice clean-cut guy or a possessive maniac?

Silja reiterated the argument Alexis had had with Monroe just that afternoon. Detective Landry wrote the information on his notepad, making sure he got the spelling of Monroe's name correct, what role she danced in the ballet, and what position she held in the company. Silja went on to inform him that they had seen Monroe go into the next dressing room directly after they'd found Alexis's body. He had no reaction to that information. It was probably all part of murder police training.

Finally, the questioning grew to a close. "Do you know anything about her family?"

Sighing, Silja shrugged. "I know that her parents were killed in a car accident a year or so ago. She and I have that in common, unfortunately. If she had any brothers or sisters, she's never mentioned them to me."

"Thank you for your cooperation, ladies. We're gathering the staff, stage crew, and the cast in the auditorium for questioning. Would you please come along? I'd like you to point out Ms. McCarthy, if you would."

"What about the show?" Silja inquired.

"It's been cancelled for tonight, perhaps even tomorrow's show will be cancelled. The theater is a crime scene, Ms. Ramsay. I don't know if they'll give refunds or reschedule the performances," he explained as he stuffed his pen behind his ear, and they made their way down the hallway toward the auditorium.

Fiona paused a moment at the door where she'd seen the old woman come out. It was marked, *maintenance*. The woman must work as a janitress.

"Coming, Fiona?" Silja called back to her. Fiona quickened her step to catch up. The Benedum seemed so exposed with all the lights illuminated It didn't have the enigmatic aura about it as when the lights were dimmed and a performance was about to begin. The phantoms of the theater were absent now, faded away into the walls and the corners. Perhaps they didn't appreciate the bright lighting or the police probing into their private spaces.

The curtains and backdrops had been lifted, revealing the entire backstage area. And while the police did an extensive search of the theater, there were so many places to hide in the huge building that Fiona could only assume they were trying to eliminate as many as possible.

The seats in the auditorium were filled with ushers, members of the stage crew, vendors, dancers, and way in the back sat the janitorial staff. Fiona recognized a member of the cleaning staff—the old woman from the garage. The red scarf wrapped around her shoulders, now served as a shawl. She kept to herself, not talking with anyone. Calvin walked along the back of the seats, stopping by each person to talk for a moment and then he would move to the next. When he reached the woman, he knelt down. It was then she noticed he'd brought her the pain medication and a bottle of water. He spoke with her for a longer period of time than anyone else. She smiled at him and patted his hand, before he rose to find a seat amongst his crew.

Did the murder frighten her? She decided to make a point to talk with her after the police excused them, and perhaps offer to walk with her back to the garage. Detective Landry was taking note of Calvin's interest in the old woman as well. Then again, the detective seemed to be watching everyone.

The room hummed with conversation about Alexis Cartwright's awful demise. Most of the dancers were wearing street clothes or comfy sweats as they had been informed of the cancelled show, except for Monroe. She swept into the auditorium still sporting her Coppelia costume, only her lovely red hair cascaded about her shoulders, instead of in the taut bun required for the performance, and she wasn't wearing the mandatory doll-like makeup for the role.

Silja hitched her chin in Monroe's direction to identify her for Detective Landry, he nodded in reply. The detective stopped her before she got too far away.

"Excuse me, Miss…"

Monroe turned to face the detective, feigning a pleasant smile.

"I'm Detective Nathan Landry. I have a lot of people to talk to here, but since you're so close, do you mind if I question you first?"

"Well, okay, if it'll get me out of here faster," Monroe said, glancing in Fiona and Silja's direction.

Detective Landry opened his jacket to look in the inside pocket. "Your name is?"

"Monroe McCarthy, I'm a soloist. I'm dancing the role of Coppelia for this production. I feel so badly for what happened to Alexis." Suddenly Monroe blinked back. Letting out a loud huff, she planted her hands on her hips while watching the detective patting his chest and the front pockets of his slacks.

Looking up, he pitched her a bashful smile. "Do you have a pen I could borrow? I think the perp from earlier today kept mine after signing his statement."

Rolling her eyes, Monroe opened her arms wide. "Just where would I keep a pen, Detective Landry?" And then her eyes flicked to his head. "Besides, you have one tucked behind your ear."

"Oh, thanks. See there? I automatically suspect my suspects. Nasty habit."

"I suppose it comes with the territory."

"I suppose you're right, Ms. Monroe—"

"McCarthy, my first name is Monroe—*Monroe McCarthy*."

He leaned in close. "It is *really*? Or is that one of those…um…stage names?"

Monroe's nostrils flared. Her shoulders and spine stiffened. Her glare was so abrasive that Fiona was waiting for poisonous daggers to shoot out of her pupils at the detective. She couldn't believe how patiently he waited for her reply. He stared at her like he was in a trance—like he was so mesmerized by her beauty that he could barely concentrate.

Through gritted teeth, Monroe finally managed, "Do you have any *real* questions for me, Detective?"

He blinked back, and then pulling out his notepad, he cleared his throat. "I'm sorry. Of course I do. When was the last time you saw Ms. Cartwright alive?"

"After the early show, before I left for lunch."

Detective Landry made a clucking sound with his lips, while making a big show of quickly flipping back through the crinkled papers of his notepad. He stopped, read, and scratched his head. With furrowed brows, he looked up at her. "Ummm, that's not quite right, Ms. *McCarthy*. It says here in my notes that you were seen coming out of the theater, and then you went right back in. Could you have possibly gone back to the dressing room to finish your quarrel with Ms. Cartwright, or possibly do harm to her?"

Monroe's eyes widened. She took in a gasp. "I never touched the woman!"

"But you did argue with Ms. Cartwright?"

"Well…we just didn't get along very well, that's all."

"Because she was a main dancer and you're not?"

"You mean she was a *principal dancer,* and I'm a soloist?"

"I guess that's what I meant. You were jealous of Ms. Cartwright?"

"Absolutely not! Our personalities clashed. We just didn't get along."

He continued to jot down her statements. "Okie, dokie. Why did you go back into the theater?"

"I didn't…oh, yes, I—I forgot my cell phone. I went back to get it. Alexis was alive when I went back in and when I came back out."

Peering up at her, Detective Landry took down what she said and shrugged. "Whatever you say, Ms. McCarthy. I don't have any evidence that proves otherwise." With a loud *harrumph*, she whirled around to walk away. He added, "Yet."

Hearing his last remark, Monroe turned back to face him with a scowl, and then marched through the narrow channel between the orchestra pit and the front row seats. As she passed Fiona and Silja, she snarled, "I know exactly who told that *moron* I went back into the theater!"

Three

It had been a long drawn out evening. When Detective Landry excused everyone, Fiona looked for the old woman she'd met that afternoon, but couldn't find her anywhere. She hoped she had made it back to her vehicle safely.

Rolling her car to a stop in front of her house, Fiona was thankful to be home. The flurry from earlier in the day had laid down a quick inch of snow. The sidewalk leading up to her house was covered. She would have to take extra care not to slip in her high-heels. She also took note that the porch light was on. No, she hadn't left a light on because she wasn't expecting to arrive home so late. She knew who'd turned the light on for her.

Fiona lived in her childhood home. Her mother also grew up in the big brick house at 529 Oxford Street with the cozy porch that stretched all the way across the front of the house. When her mom and dad retired from long teaching careers and moved to Florida two years ago, she bought the large drafty house from them. While most of her friends lived in swanky apartments, she preferred the old family home with the biggest yard on the block, and in good weather, she was able to walk the three blocks or so to the elementary school where she taught.

The house held so many memories that she simply couldn't part with, and she had a strong sense that her grandmother, Evelyn, still resided in the home as well. It wasn't just the bumps in the night that clued her in to Evelyn's presence, it was things that were moved from one place to another, and like tonight, the front porch light was on when she hadn't touched the switch. It was as if her late grandmother wanted to make sure she got into the house unscathed.

As she shoved the key into the lock, she could hear another resident of the house welcoming her home, or maybe she was reprimanding her for taking so long—Harriet, her white Maltese. Most likely the little dog had reached her limit and needed to go outside, badly. Fiona stumbled through the door to find Harriet dancing circles in her crate, while barking fiercely.

"Okay, okay, I'm home. I'm sorry," Fiona bent down to open the door to the crate. Harriet pounced out of the cage, scurried out the front door to dive off the porch into the snow, while Fiona slipped off her coat to hang it on the square fluted newel at the base of the staircase. She kicked off her heels and set them on the first step to carry up to bedroom just as Harriet came romping back into the house, and flopped down on the long floral oriental runner to wipe the snow from her coat. Fiona locked the door, then she crossed the foyer into the living room, and turned on the TV—just in time for the eleven o'clock news broadcast.

Exhausted, she dropped onto the couch. Harriet leapt onto her lap, insisting that her mistress pay her the attention she deserved after spending so much time in her crate. Fiona was more than happy to oblige the little dog, cuddling her to her chest, when the anchorman for KDKA News announced the lead story for the night. "A tragic turn of events this evening at the Benedum Center. A ballerina was found murdered in one of the dressing rooms—"

A photograph of Alexis Cartwright flashed across the screen, followed by footage of the police and the crowds outside the Benedum, while a reporter gave the gruesome details that were available thus far. After dealing with the murder up close and personal all evening, Fiona really didn't care to hear any more about it. Clicking off the TV with the remote, she hugged Harriet closer to her, and then laid her head back to close her weary eyes for just…a…few…moments—

—⚬—

Fiona woke with a start. Someone was knocking on the front door. The news was over—way over, as the time in the corner of the TV screen read, 2:00AM. The news had been replaced by a man droning on and on about how important a security system was—the one he was selling to be specific.

Another round of knocks sounded. Fiona had her own security system. It wasn't particularly sophisticated, but it definitely made a lot of noise—barking!

Running her fingers through her hair, she pushed from the couch to join her security system, Harriet, at the front door. Peering through the beveled glass, she could see the shape of a man who looked a lot like Detective Landry and a woman who looked a lot like...*Silja?*

What on Earth?

The cold night chill swept over her when she yanked the door open. Harriet bounded out the door to bark and snarl at Detective Landry and Silja who was wearing a bandage on her head.

"Oh! My goodness! What happened to you, Silja?" Fiona gasped.

"Sorry to interrupt your night, Ms. Quinn, but I didn't think Ms. Ramsay should go back to her hotel tonight. I felt she'd be better off under the care of a friend," Detective Landry explained. His brows fell into a V. "Isn't that the dress you were wearing at the theater?"

She looked down at the now wrinkled black sheath dress. "Oh, well, yes it is. I usually change into pajamas, but I fell asleep on the couch. Never mind that—" Fiona took Silja by the arm to pull her inside. "Come in. What happened?"

"It's not as bad as it looks," Silja insisted, while Fiona led her into the living room with the detective following behind. Harriet yipped, running circles around the unfamiliar visitors. The detective scooped the dog up, while Fiona eased Silja onto the couch.

"Sorry about getting snow all over your rug," the detective apologized.

"No, no, it's okay." She sat down next to Silja. "Now, what happened?"

"After you left, we had a meeting about who will dance the open parts in the ballet." Silja winced with pain. "Afterward, I went to my car to drive to the hotel, and I guess someone whacked me on the head. I really don't remember."

"This person tried to kill two ballerinas in one night? This is really scary," Fiona said.

"We definitely have an over-achiever on our hands," the detective responded. "Thankfully the culprit didn't have a chance to finish the job on Ms. Ramsay. One of the dancers came along and must've scared them off. We took her to the hospital. No stitches, just some bruising, but a possible slight concussion, so she needs to take it easy." He handed the dog to Fiona. "I've assigned a police officer to sit outside the house all night to keep watch. I'll be back in the morning. I have something I want to discuss with you, Ms. Quinn."

"What would that be?"

"It can wait until morning. I think we all need to get some rest. It's been a trying day." With that he made his way to the door, but before he opened it, he turned back. "I think it would be a good idea if Ms. Ramsay stayed here with you, Ms. Quinn, until the case is closed or she returns to Harverton. It will be easier for a police officer to watch the house than a hotel room, if that's okay?"

"Silja's welcome to stay as long as she'd like."

"That's great. We'll see to it that you get your car, Ms. Ramsay. Good night, ladies."

From her spot on the couch, Fiona had a clear view through the picture window of the detective walking to his vehicle. Sure enough, a police cruiser pulled in and parked in front of her Mini Cooper.

"You kind of like him. Don't you?" Silja suggested, her lips curled into a sassy smirk.

Fiona lifted a shoulder. "He seems nice."

"He's not wearing a wedding ring."

"Already noted. Do you know what he wants to talk to me about?"

"Like the man said, it can wait until tomorrow. My head's pounding. I just want to get some sleep."

"Should we call your husband and let him know what happened?"

"I can't."

"What do you mean, you can't?"

Silja let out a sigh. "I don't know where Grant is. I'm not supposed to tell anyone this, but I know I can trust you. Grant works special ops. So he's on a mission somewhere. When he goes, I don't know where he is or when he'll be back. So no, I can't call him. He'll find out after the fact—maybe *way* after the fact."

"Oh, Silja, that's unbelievable. The not knowing—it must be hard."

"It's not easy, that's for sure. But I love him to death, and yes, I worry that he won't come home at all. But it's what he loves to do, and I signed on for the long haul, so that's the way it is."

Fiona squeezed her hand. "Can I get you anything?"

"Have you got a comfy bed? I'm exhausted. I just want to sleep."

Pulling her up from the couch, Fiona looped her arm through Silja's. "I think I can accommodate you. C'mon."

Harriet merrily led the way up the staircase, and as they climbed, Fiona heard the switch for the porch light click off. *Thanks, Ev.*

When she wasn't checking on Silja, Fiona spent most of the night staring at the bedroom ceiling, while Harriet stretched out. It was amazing how much of a queen-sized bed an eight pound dog could take up. The street lamp's light filtered through the curtains lending a soft glow to the room that used to provide a sense of comfort when she was a child, and still did sometimes, but not tonight.

Tonight, she couldn't find any solace or comfort. Was there a serial killer on the loose in Pittsburgh who had his sights set on ballerinas? Even under the warmth of her heated blanket, a shiver rolled through her. Her busy brain wouldn't let her sleep. Her mind wandered to Detective Landry. She couldn't imagine what he could possibly want to discuss with her in the morning. A glance at her clock told her it was morning, 5:00AM.

She flipped over to her right side for the hundredth time. Harriet let out a tiny whimper, letting her annoyance be known. Enough was enough. Lying in the bed was an exercise in weary futility. Tossing the blankets aside, she lifted from the bed to slide into her slippers and her robe. Completely covered by the discarded blankets, it was obvious that Harriet didn't intend to move from her cozy nest.

Trying to be as quiet as possible over the creaky old floor, Fiona made her way down the hall and the staircase. She held tightly to the dark pine handrail as the sun hadn't come up yet, and the house was still blanketed in darkness. She peered out the beveled glass on the door to see that there were now two police cruisers in front of her house. At first she was concerned, until she saw a female police officer get out of the second cruiser to deliver hot coffee to the officer in the first cruiser that had shown up last night. Well, actually, three hours ago.

Was this a girlfriend on the force or just one cop helping out another? She'd have to keep an eye on that—just for a fun distraction. She made her way to the kitchen to make some coffee. She'd left her laptop on the kitchen table so now was as good a time as any to check her emails. Her mind wandered to Detective Landry and what time he would show up to talk with her. Looking up at the clock, she figured she had several hours before that happened.

The hours ticked by slowly. She calmed her fears by answering a few emails from several concerned parents who'd heard rumors that whooping cough was going around the school, another from an old college roommate, and one from her mother who'd heard about the murder at the Benedum and wondered if Fiona had seen anything. In her reply, Fiona claimed ignorance. She told her that she'd left the Benedum before they discovered the body. She didn't want to get her mother in a dither with the knowledge that she was smack dab in the middle of the ordeal. She'd tell her mother all about it when it was over—maybe.

She emptied her spam folder.

Finally, at nine o'clock, Silja wandered into the kitchen, wearing a pair of Fiona's grey sweats. Her golden brunette hair was bed tossed and she still looked pallid from last night's bad experience, but she managed a sleepy smile, and asked, "Coffee?"

"Good morning! Did you manage to sleep?"

"Between the pounding in my head and all the noise coming from the attic, I didn't do too badly. I finally drifted off. What's all the racket up there?"

Fiona hesitated. "Um…prob'ly the furnace."

"In the *attic*?"

"Reverberation. How are you feeling?"

Silja tossed her a befuddled look, and replied, "Better, the pounding has calmed to a dull thump, so that's good. I suppose. No Detective Landry yet?"

Looking down at her robe, while brushing back her tousled hair, Fiona said, "I wouldn't think he'd show up this early, would you?"

Silja chuckled at Fiona's panicked reaction. "Don't worry, you look cute as a button in your jammies, but no, I don't think he'd come this early. Are the police still outside?"

Fiona sat a mug of coffee in front of Silja. "The changing of the guard happened about an hour ago—shift change, I'm guessing. Do you really think we need police protection? I mean, do you think the killer has certain ballerinas on his hit list? Or do you think you were in the wrong place at a convenient time?"

"Or *her* hit list. I wouldn't be one bit surprised if it was Monroe McCarthy who smacked me last night. She really wants to be a principal dancer and with Alexis out of the way, well…"

"I'm not sure if I hope you're right or wrong. All the more reason for you to tell Monroe that you're only here to dance in Coppelia, and then you're going home. Still, she seems too easy a suspect. I'm thinking we're overlooking someone. Someone who has an axe to grind with PBT or perhaps the Benedum management. Maybe someone would benefit in some way with Alexis out of the way. I mean, other than the obvious. Maybe they'd benefit from her death outside her career. It's an interesting thought."

"Look at you, coming up with scenarios. Whatta sleuth!" Silja laughed. Just then there was a knock at the door. Fiona's eyes widened. Her mouth dropped open. Harriet shot down the stairs, barking. Silja said, "Uh, oh, guess we were wrong. Looks like Detective Landry is an early riser."

"I look like a train wreck!"

"You look adorable. Go on, get the door. It'll be fine. I promise."

All the way down the hall and through the foyer Fiona was cursing herself for not getting dressed—she'd had plenty of time. For crying out loud, she'd been up since five! Why didn't she get dressed? Maybe she should've taken a shower, done her hair, maybe a little makeup.

Idiot.

Still in the midst of self-reprimand, she opened the door to find Detective Landry smiling at her. "Good morning, Detective Landry. I'm so sorry that I'm not dressed. I should've been. I've been up and about since five, but I didn't realize that you'd be so early. I don't usually stay in my pajamas so late in the morning. I mean, of course I don't. I'm a kindergarten teacher. I'm usually at school by this time. Well, not on Sundays.

There's no school on Sundays. Sometimes I stay in my pajamas a little later on Sundays." She looked beyond Detective Landry, a steady snow was compounding what was already lying on the sidewalk, lawn, and Oxford Street. "And it's a snowy Sunday to boot—"

In an elf-like voice, Silja whispered in her ear, "Help! I'm talking and I can't shut up!"

Letting out a sigh, Fiona said, "I'm sorry, please come in, Detective. Would you like some coffee?"

"Thanks, Ms. Quinn. Again, sorry about your rug. Don't worry, you look cute as a button in your jammies," he said, as he stepped into the foyer with another man behind him that Fiona hadn't noticed—she was too busy rambling like some sort of love-struck teenager.

Idiot.

"Thank you, I think." With that she closed the door and then realized who the man was that came in with Detective Landry, her old Ballet Master, David Sheppard. Fiona was impressed at how good he looked for his age. He had a sophisticated aura about him. His pure white hair blended down his sideburns into an intricately close cut beard. He was tall and lean. He still had the look of a dancer, even at sixty-five. She admired how well he portrayed the role of Dr. Coppelius.

David immediately gave Silja a kiss on the cheek. "This is such a terrible situation. I feel so badly about Alexis. I was stunned when I came back from lunch to hear the news, and I was equally as stunned when

I heard you'd been attacked, too. I'm so glad to see that you're all right, Silja. I was worried to death over you, my dear," he said, while running his hands up and down Silja's arms.

Silja stepped out of his reach. "I'm fine, David. You remember Fiona Quinn?"

David enveloped her in a hug. "Yes, of course, Fiona, my dear. So happy to see you again. You're lovely!"

Fiona pulled away, removing his hand from her right butt cheek. Yeah, she remembered that about the old Ballet Master too. "Good to see you too, David. So…what's this all about?"

"Well, I sure would like to have some of that coffee. Where can we talk? In the kitchen? Or would you prefer the living room? Wherever is most comfortable for you on this snowy Sunday morning," Detective Landry said.

"Have a seat in the living room. Silja and I will get the coffee."

Silja followed Fiona into the kitchen. "What's David doing here?" Fiona asked as she pulled a tray from the pantry and placed several mugs on it.

"You'll see."

Fiona gave her a look, and then poured coffee into the mugs, while Silja gathered up the sugar and the creamer from the table. "Why don't you just tell me? What's the secrecy all about?"

"The detective needs your help, and I'm hoping you won't turn him down."

"I'm not sure I like the sound of this."

After serving the coffee, Fiona and Silja took their seats. Harriet was more than comfortable on Detective Landry's lap. Fiona was still wishing she'd at least thrown on a pair of old jeans and a sweatshirt this morning.

"Okay, what's going on? What's David doing here? And what does it all have to do with me, Detective?" Fiona inquired.

"We'd like you to return to the stage, Ms. Quinn. We'd like you to take the role of Coppelia until we have this murder solved or the ballet comes to a close—whichever happens first. I'm hoping to close the case. Ms. McCarthy will be dancing Alexis Cartwright's part."

Fiona was speechless. Slowly her eyes flicked from the detective to Silja to David, and then back to the detective. "I can't dance the part of Coppelia. I haven't danced in years! I doubt I could get my feet into a pair of pointe shoes let alone dance in them! Surely Pittsburgh has a police officer who could do this, who has danced at some point in her life."

"Well, our dispatcher, Millie Atwell mentioned that she used to dance, but that was twenty years and thirty pounds ago. Look, PBT is on board with this. Mr. Sheppard plays the role of Dr. Coppelius, and he's more than willing to teach you the part of Coppelia."

Fiona glanced at David who was smiling at her like the Cheshire Cat. She asked, "What's the purpose of me dancing the role? What am I supposed to do?"

"You'd basically be going undercover for us. You'd be on the inside of the cast, able to keep up with what's going on. We'd use Silja, but her role is more demanding. You'll have a better opportunity to keep an eye on everyone and report anything suspicious."

"I don't know—"

"Don't worry, you'll be safe. We have police in amongst the stage crew."

"Since the weekend performances were cancelled, we have a full week before the next performance, Fiona. You'll have plenty of time to learn your cues and the doll dance," Silja cajoled.

"You're forgetting that I'm a teacher. I have to be at school all day. When would I rehearse?"

"David is going to rehearse with you in the evening in one of the studios at Pittsburgh Ballet School—where we used to dance, and then we'll have a special dress rehearsal Thursday night at the Benedum, for the entire cast. After all, there will be dancers performing in different roles so it will give everyone a chance to regroup. C'mon, it'll be like old times, Fiona, it'll be fun."

"Fun isn't exactly what I had in mind, Ms. Ramsay," the detective broke in. "I need Fiona…er… Ms. Quinn, to pay attention to conversations around her. Pay attention to how the dancers are interacting. I don't mean to be a party pooper, and by all means enjoy your return to dance and the stage but be on the lookout at the same time."

"Soooo…are you in, Fiona?" Silja asked.

Fiona stared at her feet as if the answer to Silja's question lay on the floor between them. She didn't want to let down Alexis Cartwright, Detective Landry, or the city of Pittsburgh, but she just wasn't sure she could handle teaching twenty-five rambunctious kindergarteners all day and then dancing all evening—on pointe shoes, no less. She also wasn't too sure about stepping onto the Benedum's stage after such a long absence. Scary.

Taking in a beleaguered breath, she dragged her gaze to meet Silja's, and then Detective Landry's. "I'm in," she said.

Silja threw her arms around Fiona. "It's going to be so wonderful dancing with you again! I'll bet you fall in love with performing all over again! You'll see!"

"Maybe," Fiona muttered, but she wasn't convinced—at all.

Four

Monday proved to be a challenging day with Fiona's kindergarten class. She wasn't sure what was in the air, but the children were more disorderly than usual. It wasn't even ten o'clock when one of the girls in her class stuffed crayons up her nose. The child had to be sent to the nurse's office to have them removed.

Fiona had arranged for the kids to paint on their easels in the afternoon. Two boys got into a paint fight. Their mothers were not happy when they were called to pick the boys up early.

"You should learn to control your classroom, Ms. Quinn," one of the mothers growled on her way out the door. While mommy number two moaned, "I hope Jayden doesn't get a rash from all this paint on his skin. He's very sensitive, you know."

Ugh!

She was thankful when her planning period rolled around. She gladly sent the class to the music teacher, then went to the office to pick up a package that had been sent to her from the shoemaker at PBT—her pointe shoes. This was really happening. She was really going to tie on a pair of pointe shoes and dance on the Benedum stage.

She swallowed hard. *What have I gotten myself into?*

By the time the children were on their buses for the ride home, Fiona was all but used up, physically and emotionally. Gathering up her backpack filled with a leotard, tights, ballet sweater, and the box containing her new pointe shoes, she brushed her fingers through her hair, stretched her back, and then made her way down the hallway toward the teacher's parking lot. She would need to make a quick stop at home to let Harriet out of her crate for a much needed visit outside, then she would be off to PBT located on Liberty Avenue in downtown Pittsburgh. She wasn't looking forward to the drive.

Checking the time on her cell phone, she let out a groan. She was just in time for the crazy traffic at the Fort Pitt Tunnels. She could travel via the West End Circle, but she doubted that the traffic situation would be any less forgiving.

If she were being honest, she truly was looking forward to working out at the ballet barre again. She was ready for chaine turns across the floor, while the pianist played a lively tune on the baby grand in the far corner of the studio. What she wasn't looking forward to was the aching muscles that would be screaming at her when she rolled out of bed in the morning. What she was terrified of was slipping her feet into the pointe shoes—the blisters, the blood, and the pain that she knew would accompany the aggravated muscles.

Back in the day, David Sheppard was a demanding Ballet Master. She had no recollection of the man showing any mercy to the dancers with sore feet or muscles. Maybe he'd mellowed in his old age. She could hope, anyway.

After giving Harriet ten minutes on the snow laden lawn, she stuffed the frustrated Maltese back into her crate and hurried out the door. She decided to take her chances with the West End Circle—it was a closer route anyway.

As anticipated, the traffic was brutal, yet thirty minutes later, Fiona was pulling into the parking lot at the ballet school. She wasn't late. She was relieved that she had approximately fifteen minutes to get dressed before her rehearsal with David. They had until Friday to pull it all together.

The lot was packed. It was prime time for classes to begin for school-aged dancers, but she was in luck, a woman was backing out of a space next to a silver Mercedes parked close to the entrance. She waited patiently for the woman to pull out, and then she rolled into the spot. She was careful not to let her door bump the Mercedes as she eased out of her car.

The Mini Cooper let out a *beep beep* as she pressed the lock on her keyring and slung her backpack over her shoulder to walk toward the door.

Hesitating, she turned to look at the vehicle parked next to hers—a silver Mercedes.

Wait a minute.

Could it be the same Mercedes that Monroe was going to get into before she changed her mind and went back into the theater?

Did Detective Landry ask Monroe who she was going to lunch with? She couldn't remember. This was the kind of information that the detective was looking for, no doubt. First, she had to find out who the Mercedes belonged to. Quickly, she dug through her backpack for her cell, snapped a picture of the vehicle, and then hurried to get a shot of the license plate.

Pushing through the door, she found the receptionist desk just inside—like it had always been. She found a strange comfort in the fact that some things hadn't changed.

The receptionist smiled. "Can I help you?"

"I'm here to rehearse with David Sheppard."

"You must be Fiona. He's in Studio D. Down the hall and to the left. It's a smaller studio, but it should do nicely. The locker room is off to your right, if you need to change."

"Thank you." A shudder of nerves ran through her. She was tenser than she'd realized. Half way across the lobby she stopped and turned back to the receptionist. "Do you know who owns the silver Mercedes parked outside?"

"I'm sorry, no. Is it blocking someone in? I could make an announcement."

"No, no, I was just wondering who's it might be. Thank you." Fiona made her way to the dancer's locker room to change. As soon as she was dressed, she sat on the bench to send a text to Detective Landry with the photos she'd taken of the Mercedes.

She looked down at the box that contained the pointe shoes lying on the bench. It was time. There was no avoiding the inevitable. She removed the lamb's wool that the shoemaker had provided to wrap her toes. On a braced breath she slipped the shoes on her feet. Instantly, her heart filled with warmth at the memory of dancing in the beloved shoes. She remembered the joy of the first time she pressed up onto the box, and the thrill the moment she managed her first pirouette. Silja was right. It was still there—locked away deep in her heart. The feeling had been asleep, and now with the shoes on her feet, and her hands twisting the ribbons around her ankles, it had awakened. Unerringly she tied the ribbons into a knot on the inside of her ankle. It was like riding a bike, her fingers seemed to know how to tie it. Fiona smiled. She was ready to face her old Ballet Master, David Sheppard.

Thank God she hadn't let her muscles go to flab. Fiona worked out at the gym twice per week, participated in a Zumba class, and on the weekends she attended a yoga class. Placing her leg on the barre for long slow stretches wasn't nearly as painful as she had imagined.

Her toes weren't too keen on the idea of rolling up onto the hard boxes inside the pointe shoes, but she managed to pull up into releve and balance. Yay!

Moving down the floor proved to be a bit more of a challenge. She fell off the shoes several times when attempting chaine turns across the floor that seemed like a mile wide. It was amazing how she automatically spotted the corner—no, she hadn't forgotten that either.

"Not bad, Fiona. Not bad at all for someone who hasn't danced in ten years and is closing in on thirty," David remarked.

"Twenty-eight, I'm twenty-eight," Fiona supplied from her seated position on the floor. She needed a little break, and she was most grateful that David actually allowed her to have one—ten years ago it would have been unheard of. Her face was flushed with sweat. She could feel it dribbling down between her shoulder blades, and yet the old Ballet Master didn't have so much as a glisten of moisture on his brow.

David offered her his hand to help her to her feet, and again she was taken aback by his compassion. Perhaps he had mellowed. Lucky for her.

"I know that you're tired, but take heart, my dear. We're going to do a little cheating."

"What do you mean?"

"Well, you haven't danced on pointe shoes or been on stage in many years, and we only have until Friday to pull this all together. So, we're going to make adjustments to the choreography of the doll dance." Leaving her standing in the middle of the studio, David made his way to the door, stepped into the hallway, and then returned dragging a chair. He placed it next to her, gesturing for her to have a seat. "We're going to start the dance in the chair, keep you in it for as long as possible, and then return you to it by the end of the dance." Fiona let out a sigh of relief. Just then David's cell phone rang. He pulled it from the pocket of his jazz pants. "Hello...I'll be home a bit late. I'm still rehearsing. I'll talk with you later, Cynthia."

Shoving the phone back into the pocket, he seemed annoyed by the interruption. Fiona said, "Cynthia Montgomery...I'd forgotten that you were married to her. She retired before I had an opportunity to work with her or have her as a teacher."

"Yes...my Cynthia was a celebrated principal dancer for many years until the accident."

"How is she nowadays?"

"Not well, I'm afraid. She's become an old woman, bitter, disengaged. I find her—" Blinking back, he waved a dismissive hand in the air. "I don't want to talk about it. We have work to do, so let's get to it, shall we? Please have a seat, Fiona. Hands in your lap, knees together, roll up on the shoes, and a vacant look on your face. Remember, you're a doll."

"Yes, of course." Fiona murmured, as she lowered her tiring body onto the chair, getting into the position that David requested. She recalled some of the dolls that her students had brought to class over the years for "show and tell." Using the dolls as a mental picture, she puckered her lips, widened her eyes, and cocked her head to one side.

"Perfect!" David exclaimed.

She was happy that David was pleased with her work and her interpretation of Coppelia, yet throughout the rest of the rehearsal, she couldn't put Cynthia Montgomery out of her mind. The ballerina had been the pride of Pittsburgh until she was hit by a car on Seventh Street after a performance many years ago. Among other serious injuries, her legs had been badly broken, ending her illustrious career.

It was shortly after the accident that David gave up his position at PBT, and the couple moved away. Rumor had it that Cynthia never wanted to step foot in the city ever again. Why would David accept a role in Pittsburgh, and how did he get the former ballerina to return?

When rehearsal finally ended, Fiona was exhausted, and even though she wasn't required to dance on pointe every step of the choreography, she knew that her feet and muscles would be protesting every move that she made tomorrow.

When she stepped out of the locker room, David was making his way through the lobby, while shrugging into his black coat. Fiona hurried to catch up.

"David…" He turned. "Does Cynthia come to the performances?"

"She's usually at the Benedum during them, yes."

"I would love to meet her. Would you introduce me?"

He stilled. She could sense his reluctance. His lip twitched, and then he said, "I suppose I could." Tugging his black and tan plaid muffler to his chin, David held the door open for Fiona to step into the blustery evening, only to find Detective Landry circling the Mercedes.

"Hello, Ms. Quinn," he nodded. "And Mr. Sheppard. Nice car."

"Thank you, Detective," David said, raising a brow.

Uh, oh, the Mercedes belongs to David. Should she hurry to her car and drive away, or should she remain on the sidewalk to see the outcome of the conversation?

She stepped off the sidewalk and then stilled. Hey, she was the one who reported the Mercedes to the detective. She should stay to see what he was going to do, right?

Absolutely.

She hunkered down deeper into the collar of her coat, pushing her hands deeper into the pockets to watch and learn.

After letting out a long downward whistle, the detective said, "Looks expensive."

"Oh yes, these Mercedes aren't cheap." The car beeped after David hit the unlock button, while quickly making his way toward the driver's side door.

"I'll bet. I couldn't afford one of these on my salary that's for sure. I've never seen the inside of one of these. Do you mind if I check it out?"

David hesitated, and then gave him the nod.

Smiling, Detective Landry leaned inside the car. "How many miles to the gallon do ya get on this bad boy?"

David shifted from one foot to the other. "Oh, I dunno, twenty-seven/twenty-eight miles, of course those are city miles. On the highway she probably would get better."

"Prob'ly." Looking down on the floor, his eyes narrowed. "Uh, oh, that's a shame," he said, clucking his tongue on the roof of his mouth.

"What's that?"

"Seems you've got a little stain on the carpet here."

David hurried around the vehicle, almost slipping in the snow, to look over the detective's shoulder. "Really? Where?"

"Right there in the middle of the floor mat. Can't tell for sure, but it kind of looks like blood." Pushing the detective aside, David peered into the car, searching for the stain. Leaning against the car, Detective

Landry crossed his arms across his chest. "Cut yourself shaving, didja?"

"Well of course not! I—I don't know where that came from. You can't be sure that its blood!"

"You're right." Detective Landry took out his cell phone, and tapped out a text with his thumb. "We'll have to test it to know for sure."

"What do you mean?"

"I mean, a forensics team will have to test the spot to see if it is indeed blood, and if it is, we need to identify whose blood it is." He stuffed the cell phone back in his jacket. "They're on their way now."

"What?"

"Who did you have a lunch date with the day of Alexis Cartwright's murder? With your wife or Monroe McCarthy?"

"How did you know that I'm—what makes you think that I went out to lunch that day?"

"Answer to question one: you're wearing a wedding ring, dead giveaway that you're married. And the answer to question two: you told me. You mentioned going out to lunch the day of Ms. Cartwright's murder when we were at Ms. Quinn's home yesterday morning. So who did you have lunch with? Your wife or Ms. McCarthy?"

"What makes you think I had lunch with Monroe?"

"Because she was seen getting into a silver Mercedes after the early performance," he said with a sweep of his hand, indicating the car sitting before them.

"I'm quite sure this isn't the *only* silver Mercedes in Pittsburgh, Detective Landry!"

"Oh, I'm sure you're right, Mr. Sheppard, but this one has a suspicious stain on the floor mat, so as my mom always said, 'better safe than sorry', 'course she was referring to condoms, but I'm thinkin' this still applies."

Fiona couldn't smother the chuckle that forced its way to her lips. She turned away so David didn't see her amusement. At this point, a group of students stepped out of the building.

"I believe you have to have a warrant to search my car. Isn't that right?" David asked.

"Well, yeah, I suppose so. I could make a call if you want and get one here within thirty minutes or so." He put his hand up in a halting manner. "Now don't get me wrong, Mr. Sheppard, you are well within your rights to refuse. But if you do, and I'm not saying that you will, one would automatically think, what is Mr. Sheppard hiding? Why doesn't Mr. Sheppard want us to make absolutely sure that is not a blood stain on *his* car's mat?"

David scrubbed his fingers over his forehead. "Alright, alright, go ahead, check the stain for goodness sake."

"Thank you, Mr. Sheppard. Here they are now," the detective announced.

David turned with wide eyes and a slackened jaw at the sight of a tow truck pulling into the lot. The students stopped to watch. "I thought you said a forensic team was coming to look at the car!" David bellowed.

The detective snorted. "Oh, I think you misunderstood. They *transport* the car to their lab to analyze the contents of the vehicle—like the blood stain on your mat. They don't make house calls. You do watch TV, don't you, Mr. Sheppard?"

Fiona cupped her hand over her mouth, while watching David's face contort and twist in horror as the tow truck driver attached chains to his Mercedes, and then pressed the lever in his truck to wench the vehicle onto the flatbed.

"How long will this take?" David gasped.

"Oh, I dunno, couple hours, couple days, it depends on how backed up they are," Detective Landry said. "I could drive you back to your hotel or wherever you're staying. I'd like to meet Mrs. Sheppard, ask her a few questions about Saturday."

"No! I'm sure Fiona will drive me, won't you, Fiona?"

Fiona's eyes snapped to the detective's. His lips curled as if he knew a secret, but she was taking the subtle smile as a 'go ahead.' David turned to her with pleading eyes. She said, "Of course, David. I'll take you."

"Thank you, Fiona." He turned back to the detective. "I'm holding the city responsible if I find so much as a hint of a scratch on that car!"

The detective smiled in reply.

The tow truck driver shoved a clip board at him. "Sign here," he said around the cigarette dangling from his lip. After David signed, the driver tore a slip from the paper and handed it to him. "Claim slip, you'll need this when you pick it up." With that the tow truck driver hurried back to the truck to drive away.

With a loud *harrumph*, David turned away from the man and his Mercedes now held hostage. "Let's go, Fiona. I've had quite enough of this!"

Making their way toward her Mini Cooper, Fiona glanced over her shoulder at the detective. He was still smiling.

Five

The ten minute drive from Liberty Avenue to the William Penn Hotel was quiet, other than the din of the infamous Pittsburgh traffic. Fiona could feel the stress permeating from the man in the passenger seat across the small cab of the Mini Cooper. Was David worried that they would indeed discover Alexis's blood in his car or was he desperately trying to figure how it got there? If it was her blood, how deep was he involved in her demise?

A shiver that had nothing to do with February's wrath shuddered through her. Was there a murderer in her car? Or at the very least, an accomplice to a murder? She wasn't so sure that she wanted to know the answer. David hardly seemed to fit the murderer profile, but people do things they wouldn't normally do when pushed, and if he was pushed, what hand did Alexis have in her own death?

Fiona had a white knuckle grip on the steering wheel, while she stared at the bumper of the car in front of hers. She felt her right eyebrow involuntarily arch at her thoughts.

Then again, was it Alexis who pushed him or was it Monroe McCarthy? Fiona scolded herself silently. She was suspecting Monroe because Silja believed her to be involved—not necessarily so. Monroe was abrasive and very open about not getting along with Alexis. She was even straightforward about wanting as equal a position as Alexis at PBT, but that didn't prove she had anything to do with the dancer's death, or smacking Silja over the head.

Scary.

It was true. They had a list of suspects, but were they the correct people, or was there someone out there lurking in the shadows who had an agenda far more sinister?

"The hotel is coming up on the right. You can come to the room to meet Cynthia, if you like. I suppose now is as good as any other time. The valet will park your car," David said, breaking through her musing.

Fiona was always in awe of the William Penn Hotel. It was one of Pittsburgh's most prestigious destinations. The huge fountain was lit up in front of the grand old structure. She pulled up to the main entrance and the valet approached her car.

"Charge this to my room," David told the valet, as he and Fiona made their way toward the door. Once inside, the hotel did not disappoint. The lobby burst with welcoming elegance—gilded crown molding around floor to ceiling arched windows adorned with gold swag draperies. The grand piano softly played a classical piece. Fabulous crystal chandeliers hung from the ceiling.

David must have noticed her amazement. "You've never been?"

"No…it's beautiful."

Taking her elbow with the palm of his hand, he guided her toward the elevator. "Yes, I had to book it to get Cynthia to return to Pittsburgh. I also rented her a car so she could go shopping if she'd like. I even—" He shook his head. "It doesn't matter."

Stepping into the elevator, Fiona said, "I'm sorry, I had heard rumors that she never wanted to return to Pittsburgh."

"Not a rumor—truth. Did you know that Coppelia was the last ballet she performed before the accident?"

"No I didn't know. I also heard that they never caught the person who hit her."

The doors slid open. David stepped into the hallway. "Again, truth. It's a shame that they never arrested the person who destroyed a woman's soul."

Fiona felt ill at ease when they arrived at the room. "During rehearsal you told me Cynthia had become bitter, *disengaged*. Do you think she'll mind me dropping in unannounced?"

David lifted a shoulder as he swiped the keycard through the lock. "Who knows? It will depend on her mood. Honestly, I never know what to expect."

On a braced breath, Fiona followed him through the door. David shrugged out of his coat and muffler, tossing them on the nearest queen-size bed. "Cynthia! Where are you, my dear?"

The bathroom door opened and a woman stepped out. Her long slender body was draped in a floor-length white satin robe. Dark hair splashed with silver strands cascaded about her shoulders. Holding a glass of red wine in her left hand, she leaned heavily on a lovely blue cane with a sophisticated, braided pewter collar with the right. Slowly she made her way toward the over-stuffed chair near the bed by the window. David went to the mini bar. He took down a bottle of scotch from the glass shelf.

As Cynthia eased into the chair, she looked up to notice Fiona lingering near the door. The moment their eyes met, Fiona recognized her—Cynthia Montgomery-Sheppard, the ballerina whom she'd always admired, but more than that, she was also the old woman she'd met in the parking garage Saturday afternoon.

Fiona let out a gasp before she could call it back. For a moment she thought she could be mistaken. The woman before her looked far more refined than the woman in the parking garage. She wasn't wearing the oversized wool coat or the red scarf draped over her head, rather she was now clad in an elegant robe. In the soft lighting of the room, her face didn't look as aged, but there was no denying it—this was indeed the same woman.

The edges of Cynthia's lips curled as she swirled the wine in the glass. "I remember you. You were in the parking garage Saturday afternoon. You were very kind to me." She lifted the glass to her nose, took a whiff of the wine, and then a sip.

Waiting for an introduction, Fiona's eyes flicked to David, but he was busy searching for a glass for his scotch. Clearing her throat, she said, "Yes ma'am, my name's Fiona Quinn. I'm so pleased to meet you."

"Fiona Quinn…are you the young lady who will be dancing to role of Coppelia?"

"Oh! Cynthia, this is Fiona Quinn. She's the one who is going to take Monroe's place as Coppelia," David broke in with a careless wave of his hand and a svelte smile when he'd located just the glass he wanted.

"Thank you, David. So how did rehearsal go this evening?" she inquired.

Fiona let out a nervous giggle. "I haven't danced in a very long time—in pointe shoes, well I haven't danced at all actually—not since I ripped my meniscus almost ten years ago, but all in all, I think rehearsal went well. Don't you, David?"

There was a knock at the door.

"As well as can be expected, I suppose," he muttered as he made his way across the room.

Fiona stepped aside as David opened the door. Hesitantly, Cynthia took another sip of the wine and then directed her attention to the man at the door, prompting Fiona to do the same.

David blinked back the moment the door swung open to reveal their visitor. Irritation instantly filled his tone. "Detective Landry, what are *you* doing here?"

"I thought I'd stop by to talk with Mrs. Sheppard. Like I said before, I'd like to ask her a few questions about Saturday afternoon. I don't mean to intrude, but—"

"Cynthia is feeling a bit tired—" David attempted to close the door.

The detective caught it with his hand. "I'm feeling a little rundown myself. I think I might be coming down with a cold." Letting out a frustrated breath, David gestured for him to enter. The detective continued, "I'll have to call my mom to get some of her famous chicken noodle soup—always does the trick." His mouth turned upward when his eyes met Fiona's. "Hello again, Ms. Quinn."

"Where does your mother live, Detective?" Fiona asked.

"Monroeville."

"That's all very nice, Detective, but as I told you, Cynthia isn't feeling up to questions this evening."

"I'm just fine, David. Ask away, Detective."

Tearing his gaze away from Fiona, he looked across the room to see Cynthia slowly lift her legs onto the ottoman and cross her left ankle over her right. Settling her cane against the chair, she sipped her wine.

"Landry, I'm Detective Nathan Landry, Pittsburgh Homicide Department." He made his way across the room to stand next to her chair. "Sorry to bother you, Mrs. Sheppard. Sorry to hear you're not feeling well. I won't stay long."

Cynthia smiled at him. "Montgomery—I kept my maiden name, and please, stay as long as you like, Detective Landry. You seem to be enjoying the company." Her eyes rotated toward Fiona and then back to him. Fiona could feel the immediate heat of a blush seeping into her cheeks. With a sly curl on her lips, Cynthia continued, "Can we offer you something to drink? I know you're not allowed alcohol because you're on duty, but I'm sure we could get you a cup of coffee or a soda."

"No thank you, ma'am," the detective said.

"What would you like to know?"

"Were you at the Benedum on Saturday afternoon?"

"Yes, I work there. No I didn't see or hear anything unusual or suspicious, and yes, I know that my husband likes to wine dine and...*charm* younger women slash dancers."

"*Cynthia*—" David scolded.

She shrugged in response.

"What do you do at the Benedum?" Detective Landry asked.

"I'm a janitress. I clean. That's all I'm really good for nowadays. David keeps me employed wherever we go to keep me out of trouble or busy as he puts it."

The detective flipped through his notes. "Wait a minute now. Did I interview you Saturday? I remember seeing you, but for some reason I didn't talk with you."

"No, I had a terrible headache. I left before you got to me. Oh dear, I hope I didn't do anything wrong. I'm not in *contempt* or anything, am I?"

"Well, it would've been better had you stayed. I wouldn't have to bother you now. So where were you when Ms. Cartwright's body was found?"

"The Benedum is a big place—lots of nooks and crannies to keep tidy. I have no idea exactly where I was when she was found—cleaning something somewhere, I'm sure."

Fiona shifted from one foot to the other. She was uncomfortable being in the room during the questions, and she was even more uncomfortable with Cynthia's answers. She remembered the former ballerina coming out of a maintenance room near Alexis and Silja's dressing room shortly after they'd discovered Alexis's body.

"Does that satisfy your curiosity, Detective?" David curtly inquired, still holding the door open with an expectant glare in his eyes.

"Yes, I suppose that's all I really needed. Thank you, ma'am." He made his way toward the door, but hesitated, rubbing the nape of his neck. "Ya know, I'm really not feeling too good." He turned back toward Cynthia. "You wouldn't happen to have an extra Ibuprofen or an aspirin laying around would you?"

David let out a groan of frustration.

Fiona quickly whipped her backpack from her shoulder and began rummaging through it. "I know I have a bottle of Ibuprofen in here somewhere. Teaching twenty-five rowdy kindergartners I need them on a regular basis. Not to mention how sore I'm going to be in the morning after tonight's rehearsal." Finally, she produced the bottle.

He took the bottle from her, opened it, tossing two pills in his mouth. "Thanks, Ms. Quinn." He turned to Cynthia. "Oh, by the way, are you still having trouble with a headache? Is that why Mr. Sheppard said you weren't up to talking with me?"

Furrowing her brows, Cynthia cocked her head to one side. "Headache?"

"Yeah, you had a headache on Saturday. The maintenance man, what's his name…" he snapped his fingers in the air several times as if the gesture would magically produce the man's name.

"Calvin?" Cynthia suggested.

"Yes…Calvin, he seemed *very* concerned about it. He got you an aspirin or something—the day of the murder."

"Yes, I—I had a headache. Calvin got me an Ibuprofen. He's a very nice man."

"That's what everyone says, Calvin's a nice guy. The world certainly needs people like Calvin, doesn't it, Ms. Montgomery?"

Cynthia half-smiled in reply.

"Yes, yes, Cynthia suffers with headaches and Calvin Kleppner is a nice guy. You were leaving, Detective—" David said with a sweep of his hand in the direction of the hallway.

"Oh yeah, sorry." He made his way to the door. "Nice talking with you, Ms. Montgomery. Hope your headache goes away soon."

"I'll walk down with you, Detective," Fiona said. Hurriedly, she fell in step behind him. Hesitating at the door she said, "It was an honor to meet you, Ms. Montgomery."

"Please, call me Cynthia, and the honor was all mine, my dear. Good luck with your role as Coppelia."

"I would be so thrilled if you could sit in on one of our rehearsals. Maybe you could help—"

"Perhaps I will."

With that they stepped into the hallway, the door slamming behind them. Fiona glanced askance at Detective Landry. "Hope you're feeling better tomorrow."

The right corner of his lip hitched upward.

"So...you were honored to meet the great ballerina, Cynthia Montgomery," he said as they strolled toward the elevator.

"She was a fabulous dancer in her day. Such a shame what happened. She had so much more to offer as a teacher and a mentor to young and upcoming dancers. I'm impressed that you realized who she was."

He pressed the button for the elevator. "Oh, I realized."

"Actually, this evening wasn't the first time that I've met Cynthia. I met her on Saturday, but I didn't realize who I was talking with."

"When on Saturday?"

"On my way in to the Benedum before the performance. I met her at the elevator in the parking garage. Of course I didn't recognize her—she was so bundled up in a heavy coat and scarf. I probably wouldn't have recognized her anyway—she's aged quite a bit for obvious reasons."

"I scc. So now that you've formally met her, do you think that she thinks you're one of the many dancers that her husband wants to *charm*?"

Fiona's eyes popped open. "Oh my! I hope not! I would never! I mean, I'm not interested in David. Not only is he old enough to be my father—maybe my grandfather, but he's also married."

The detective snorted. "I doubt he'd be too happy to be compared to your grandfather, but I didn't have you pictured as the type—you're a kindergarten teacher."

The elevator doors slid open. Fiona stilled. "My being a kindergarten teacher has nothing to do with it. I'm just not that kind of girl, Detective Landry."

He held his hands up, feigning surrender. "That's what I meant. But I have to wonder, are you the type of girl who'd have a cup of coffee with an off duty detective named Nathan?"

Her lips quivered. She was trying as hard as she could to suppress the girlish giggle that was forcing its way to the surface. "I think I'm that kind of girl."

"Starbucks?"

"But of course. Wait…is it okay for you to have coffee with a murder suspect?"

"Who said you were a suspect?"

"Well, aren't I?"

Nathan chuckled.

—⟨⟨⟨—

It was after nine when they arrived, but the coffee shop was still busy. After ordering, Fiona and Nathan found seats toward the back of the café. As they scooched into the booth, Fiona asked, "Is Silja a suspect?"

"I'm really not allowed to discuss an ongoing investigation, but I can set your mind at ease by saying that neither you nor Ms. Ramsay are suspects. The other dancers at PBT said that your friend and Ms. Cartwright got along very well, so I don't really have a reason to suspect her. Should I?"

Fiona choked on the first sip of her latte. "No! Absolutely not." She swallowed it down, regaining her composure. "But I imagine Monroe is on the list. David must be or you wouldn't have stopped by his hotel this evening. Although, I don't quite understand. I thought you trusted David. You asked him to help in the investigation by teaching me the role of Coppelia to keep an eye on activity inside the ballet company."

"I didn't ask Mr. Sheppard to help in the investigation. PBT assigned him to help. Finding the blood stain in his vehicle makes him a little more suspicious than when I started the investigation. Which yes, makes me uncomfortable that he's intimate with the investigation. I don't want anyone to have a leg up on me. Besides, he's the one acting all hot under the collar, not me. That said, I was more interested in visiting with Ms. Montgomery than Mr. Sheppard."

"Cynthia? But she's so physically challenged. I couldn't imagine her hurting anyone, unless—"

Nathan watched Fiona's nose crinkle. It was obvious that she was regretting what she was about to say. "Unless, what?" he inquired.

"Oh, it's nothing, I'm sure. I'm a kindergarten teacher, not a detective."

He took a sip of his coffee. "I'm more than interested in hearing another point of view. Please, continue with what you were about to say."

"Well...what was the official cause of Alexis's death?"

"The coroner determined that it was blunt force trauma to the back of the head. Ms. Cartwright was struck with something hard several times."

"Like…um…like a cane?"

"It could happen. What are you thinking?"

"I'm sure it's nothing, but the cane Cynthia was using tonight in the hotel room was not the cane she had in the parking garage on Saturday. When I saw her in the garage she was using a plain wooden cane. Tonight she had that elegant blue cane with the fancy handle."

Nathan shrugged. "It was a very nice cane. Maybe she uses the wooden cane when she goes to work."

"Yes…that makes sense, but…she didn't have the cane at all when Calvin directed her to the auditorium for you to question everyone. Where was the cane then? Why wasn't she using it?"

Nathan cocked his head. "When I first saw her at the theater she didn't have a cane. I didn't know that she used one of course. I didn't know that a cane was missing. Although I did notice that she limped severely. Thank you for pointing it out."

Fiona sipped her latte thoughtfully. "Still, I can't believe that after all this time they've never found out who hit her and left her lying on Seventh Street."

"Remember, the crime happened over twenty years ago—long before we had traffic cams at every intersection and security cameras on practically every storefront. I've reviewed the police report. Cynthia couldn't remember much, and gave the police very little to go on. She didn't see the car coming. As a matter of fact, she stepped out from between two stopped vehicles."

"So what are you saying?"

"I'm saying that essentially the accident was Ms. Montgomery's fault. They prob'ly would not have charged the driver, had they not fled the scene."

"So the person who hit Cynthia has believed all these years that they would have gone to prison?"

"Wait a minute…this person wasn't exactly innocent, Fiona. They fled the scene of a serious accident. They were basically a coward."

"No witnesses?"

"Not really—just a few old women who were too flustered to give any real details. One said it was a blue car. Her friend claimed she was mistaken that it was a green car, and another said it was silver. Sometimes, under the city street lights cars can take on different shades. That said, the first woman who said the car was blue also insisted that the car was a Chevy, but she didn't know the make."

—⁓—

When Fiona arrived home the police cruiser was parked on the street in front of her house, and so was Silja's car. Detective Landry said they would make sure it was delivered. He was a man of his word—she liked that, very much. Another point for the super cute detective.

She pushed through the front door to find Silja and Harriet on the couch snuggled up in a fleece blanket watching TV. Fiona set straight to hanging her coat on the hook inside the door. She pulled off her knit cap, placed her gloves inside the cap, and then stuffed the bundle in the sleeve of her coat. Silja clicked the TV off with the remote.

"It's after eleven o'clock, where've you been? I was about to send the police officer outside looking for you," Silja said with an edge of reprimand in her voice.

"I noticed that it's the same cop. Has anyone showed up to bring him coffee, like a female officer?"

"Fiona...what? I have no idea. Where have you been?"

Her smile stretched up to her sapphire eyes. "Having coffee."

"With *David*? Please, I'm begging you, say no—"

"No! With an emphasis on *no way*! I was having coffee with a very handsome detective named, Nathan."

Silja jumped to her feet. Both Harriet and the blanket fell from her lap to the floor. "No way!"

"Way! He's very...*interesting*."

"I'll bet. Sooo...are you going to do more than coffee? Is there dinner and a movie in the near future? Possibly a relationship?"

"Goodness, it was just coffee. I don't think we'll be getting engaged any time soon. How did your rehearsal go today?"

"Not too badly. They didn't really allow me to do much dancing because of my head, but I felt fine. How about yours?" Silja asked.

"Better than David or I expected, I think. Have you heard from your husband?"

"No, not yet."

"Are you worried?"

"I'm always worried. But I have to have faith that he'll be okay."

Just then a set of headlights brightened the front porch. Fiona's head snapped toward the window. She hurried over, pinching back the curtain to peek out at the street. Silja followed. She pumped her eyebrows at Silja as they watched a female police officer get out of a cruiser with a coffee in one hand and a takeout bag in the other.

"Yep, same female officer," Fiona whispered, as if the officers would hear her if she spoke in a regular tone.

Silja rolled her eyes. "Oh, Fiona, you really need a boyfriend."

Six

Rolling out of bed proved to be an exercise in ouch. Groaning, Fiona gingerly pushed her aching body to a standing position. She had half a notion to call in sick. Reason—she couldn't physically face twenty-five kindergartners, not the way her back, legs, and feet were crying out for mercy.

Nope.

Missing work was not part of Fiona Quinn's MO. She'd agreed to take the part of Coppelia. She knew her body would protest, and now she had to suck it up, slather on some liniment, take at least twenty ibuprofens, and face those kindergartners with a stiff upper lip—or shoulders, or back, or legs.

Looking down at the snoring lump under the covers in the middle of the bed, she actually felt a tug of jealousy that Harriet wouldn't have to move from her comfy nest to go into her crate until it was time for Silja to go to the funeral home for Alexis later in the day.

After managing to get washed up, do her hair, and find the most comfortable pair of shoes she owned, she stumbled down the stairs to find Silja sitting at the table nibbling on a piece of toast.

"Whoa, you look like you've been hit by a truck," Silja pointed out, while pouring a cup of coffee.

Fiona rubbed her lower back. "Thanks."

"Whatta great hostess—you got up early to make fresh coffee, are you going in to work?"

"I didn't make the coffee, and yes, I'm going in to work."

"You're one tough cookie. The coffee was on when I came down."

"That doesn't mean too much in this house."

Silja looked at her over her cup. "What's that supposed to mean? And what's with all the noises coming from the third floor? Sounds like someone's up there rearranging furniture. And I thought most furnaces were located in the basement, so please don't say it was the furnace banging around. Do you have a renter or a hostage you didn't tell me about?"

Fiona tensed. She was accustomed to the bumps in the night that came from the old attic apartment where Evelyn lived for many years, but she never thought she'd have to share the information with anyone. "Oh, I wouldn't worry about it. It's nothing."

Silja leaned forward on her elbows. "That's a lot of noise for nothing, and I don't think it's *reverberation* from the furnace. Seriously, is someone up there?"

Fiona lifted a shoulder. "Well, kind of…"

"What do you mean, *kind of*? Who's up there?"

"My grandmother, Evelyn. She lives up there."

Silja sat straight up. "Your *grandmother*? She hasn't come down stairs since I've been here."

"Oh, I'm sure she has."

"Is she a recluse?"

Fiona cleared her throat, while pouring coffee into her travel mug. "She's way beyond that, I'm afraid."

"Wait a minute. Are you saying what I think you're saying?"

Fiona crinkled her face. "Most likely."

Silja looked down at her coffee cup and then back at Fiona. "Okay…so…if you didn't make the coffee… who did?"

In reply, Fiona glanced up at the ceiling and then back at Silja, whose jaw had dropped so far open that Fiona feared she'd have to pick it up from the kitchen floor. Smirking into her chest, she made her way into the foyer.

Silja pushed from the chair to follow. "Now I'm totally freaked out."

"Don't be. She's harmless. I promise." Fiona chuckled. She lifted her coat from the hook just inside the door, then pulled the knit cap from the sleeve, her gloves from inside the cap, and began to dress for the cold.

Watching the procedure, Silja rolled her eyes. "Oh, Fiona, you are such a kindergarten teacher."

Fiona stilled mid-chore of buttoning her coat. "What? Why does everyone keep pointing out that I'm a kindergarten teacher?"

"Maybe because you act so much like one."

"Aw, c'mon, it's simply a great way to keep your stuff together. Well, I guess I do preach it to the children. I should follow my own rules. Shouldn't I?"

"I dunno. What does *Evelyn* think?"

———✦———

Detective Landry followed the sound of the baby grand piano playing as he made his way along the passageways that wound through the dressing rooms to the stage area of the Benedum. Finally he arrived at the door marked "maintenance" just beyond the dressing room where Alexis Cartwright had been murdered. Leaning in, he listened, and then knocked on the door.

"C'mon in," a man's voice called from inside.

The detective pushed through the door to find Calvin Kleppner with his legs propped up on a metal desk, talking on a cell phone. The desk was old but kept in neat order. The right corner held an inbox filled with just a few papers and right next to it was a jar of peppermints. The room was rather plain. The walls were painted a dull white and an old beige carpet with several tiny red stains covered the floor. Detective Landry's eyes flicked to the metal waste can next to the desk. It was half-full with crinkled papers, a discarded Styrofoam coffee cup, a half-full bottle of rubbing alcohol, and an empty five ounce bottle of red wine.

Kicking his legs off the desk, Calvin gestured for the detective to wait for a moment. "Have a good day, and I'll look forward to seeing you soon," he told the person on the other end of the conversation before terminating the call. Smiling, he reached for the detective's hand. "What can I do for you, Detective…? I'm sorry, I've forgotten you name."

"Landry, I thought I'd stop in to talk with you a little about a member of your maintenance crew, Cynthia Montgomery."

Calvin's wide smile stretched even further. "Ahhh, yes, Cynthia. Such a sweet woman. Why would you want to talk about her?"

Detective Landry pointed to the jar of peppermints on Calvin's desk. "Would you mind?"

"No, help yourself, Detective." Removing the lid, he held the jar out.

"Thank you. I just love peppermints—clear your sinuses."

"Really?"

"Sure do—mine anyway. Ms. Montgomery seems like she has a little trouble getting around. What kind of work does she do?" he asked while fumbling to unwrap the peppermint.

Calvin's expression filled with compassion for the woman. "Yes, she does struggle a bit, poor woman. I kind of know how she feels—got a bum knee myself. But I'm just a maintenance man—always have been. To see Cynthia now, one would never know how magnificent she once was."

"What do you mean?"

"You don't know?'

Popping the peppermint into his mouth, he said, "Tell me."

"Well, Cynthia Montgomery was a prima ballerina." He sighed. "I remember standing backstage watching her dance. My Lord, she was fantastic—breathtaking." Dropping his gaze to the floor, he wrung his hands. "I feel so badly…her career was cut short by a horrible accident. She was hit by a car, right outside the theater. The person kept going—I'm sure they were scared. They were prob'ly terrified of the repercussions." He looked up, quickly. "I mean, hitting someone with a car is a serious offense. Anyway, she just does simple jobs, no heavy lifting or scrubbing anything on her hands and knees—we manage to find stuff for her to do—mainly polishing the brass on the staircases."

"You sound like you were a fan."

"Oh yes, I don't know anyone who wasn't. I'm tellin' ya, to watch Cynthia dance was like watchin' an angel from Heaven—a gift from God."

"Was she married to David Sheppard at the time? Of the accident, I mean."

"Yep, but just barely. They were just back from their honeymoon. Terrible way to start a marriage, but he's stuck with her all these years. Not that he's Mr. Faithful or anything. He flirts with the dancers terribly, and rumor has it that he steps out with them too, if ya get my meaning. He's the one who asked us to employ her while they were in town. He likes to keep her busy, which is a good thing, I suppose. Anyway, we were happy to have her on our crew."

"I know she uses a cane, but the day of the murder I noticed that she wasn't using it."

"Oh, yes. She misplaced it. We searched everywhere for it, but we never came up with it. She struggled to walk the rest of the day. It'll turn up sooner or later, I'm sure," Calvin explained.

"Hmmm, thanks for the info, Calvin, appreciate it." He turned to leave, but then turned back. "By the way, what ballet was she performing in when the accident occurred?"

"Coppelia. Kind of an interesting coincidence, isn't it? She hasn't been back to Pittsburgh since the accident that destroyed her career, and when she does return, she comes face to face with the last ballet that she performed in." He shook his head. "Man, I hope it's not bothering her too much, poor soul."

"How'd ya hurt your knee? If ya don't mind my asking—my dad had a bad knee—old football injury. Never got better."

"Oh, ah, just a fender bender years ago. Like you said, just never got better. Knees can be like that, I suppose." A cell phone buzzed. Calvin pulled it his from his pocket. "Sorry, Detective, that's my service cell. I gotta go, they need me downstairs."

"Thanks for talking with me. Have a nice day, Calvin."

Calvin hurried from the room.

The detective waited a moment, and then scooped the wine bottle up with his fingertips, delicately slipping it into his jacket pocket. He hesitated. Why would anyone throw away a perfectly good bottle of alcohol? With a shrug, he scooped it up too, and then he pulled out his cell to thumb a number.

"Hey, Mayzie, how's my gal at the DMV? Good. Hey, I need a favor—as always. Could you run a quick check for me on a Calvin Kleppner? I'd like to know what kind of vehicles he owned in the early 90's. I could run the check myself when I get back to the station, but you know me, I always want the information on the spot." He waited a moment for her reply. "Thanks, sweetheart, I owe ya one, or two thousand, but who's counting?" He chuckled at her response. "Oh, you're keeping count? Guess I owe you a coffee or two. Thanks again."

Shoving his cell into his jacket, he stepped out of the maintenance room to continue down the hallway headed for the stage. As he stepped into the backstage area, he looked out across the vast space. Some of the dancers were stretching on the ballet barre set up stage left, while others worked pirouettes, fouettes, entrechats, and other small jumps center stage, but it was David Sheppard and Monroe McCarthy who caught his attention. The two stood beyond the dancers—far stage left, engaged in an intimate conversation.

Detective Landry apologized to the agitated dancers as he made his way across the stage, interrupting their warm-ups as he traveled. "Excuse me…pardon me…oops, so sorry, Miss—"

His stumbling and stammering had David and Monroe rolling their eyes as the uninvited visitor approached.

"Mr. Sheppard…Ms. Monroe…"

"*McCarthy*, Monroe *McCarthy*," she tersely insisted.

"That's right, I keep forgetting. Prob'ly because your first name and your last name are both last names—it's kind of confusing."

Monroe let out a vexed sigh. "For some, perhaps."

David's tone was concise when he asked, "What do you need now, Detective?"

"Well, Mr. Sheppard, I got the results from the lab on that stain in your car. Turns out it wasn't blood at all—"

"Of course it wasn't! I told you it wasn't!"

"That you did. Guess I should've taken your word for it, but suspicion just wins out all the time—nasty habit."

"And—"

"And it turns out that it's a wine stain—red wine, cabernet. Are you in the habit of drinking and driving, Mr. Sheppard?"

"What? Absolutely not!"

"Well, someone was drinking in your car. Did you have wine when you went to lunch with Mr. Sheppard Saturday afternoon, Ms. McCarthy?"

"Do I need an attorney, Detective Landry?"

"Hope not."

Monroe crossed her arms over her chest. "I didn't have lunch with David on Saturday. And if I had, I wouldn't have drank any wine because I had another performance later in the day—at least I *thought* I did. In any case, we aren't permitted to drink before a performance for obvious reasons. But it doesn't matter because as I said, I didn't have lunch with David on Saturday."

The detective cocked his head to one side. "Excuse me? You were seen going to his car."

"Yes, *going* to his car, and then I went back inside for my cell phone, remember? When I came out, David was gone." She tossed David a wicked glance. "I wasn't happy, but he was gone."

"Why didn't you tell me this earlier?"

"You didn't ask, Detective."

"Okay, I'm asking now—where did you go?"

"I grabbed a quick lunch at Sal's City Deli down a couple of blocks."

"Can anyone verify that?"

Her shoulders squared, her jaw tightened, and then her eyes brightened. "Yes, that nice maintenance man…what's his name?"

"Calvin Kleppner," David supplied.

"Yes, Calvin told me about it and gave me directions. Ask him."

"I will. Where did you go, Mr. Sheppard?"

"Cynthia was having one of her episodes, migraines. I had to go back to the hotel to get her medication. You can ask the doorman, his name is Josh, we had a brief conversation." He let out a sigh, as if he were about to say something he knew he'd regret. "Anyway, by the time I got back, Monroe was gone, so I took Cynthia for a quick lunch—a very quick lunch." Monroe glowered at him all the more. David rolled his eyes in defeat.

"I see. Did Cynthia have wine in the car on Saturday?" Detective Landry asked.

"Now that's very possible. Sometimes she takes those little bottles of wine from the bar when she's cleaning up after a show."

"Mmmm, I noticed she had a cane when I visited last night. Does she always use a cane?"

"Yes, she has problems with her legs since the accident, so yes, she uses a cane."

"Interesting, because when I saw her Saturday afternoon, she didn't have a cane. She was limping down the hallway—cane-less."

"You must be mistaken. Cynthia always uses a cane. You'll have to excuse us, Detective, we're very busy. Rehearsal is about to begin." With that David palmed Monroe's elbow to escort her across the stage.

———ɷ———

Detective Landry scrubbed his fingers across his jaw while sitting in his SUV, waiting for his iPad to fire up. He picked a small Snickers bar from the cup holder, unwrapped it, and pitched it into his mouth. When the search engine appeared on the screen, he typed in *David Sheppard performances*. A nanosecond later a list of the dancer's performances for the past year were listed. His last performance was in Chicago—two months earlier. Once again he played the role of Dr. Coppelius, and four months before, he played the same role in Seattle.

Seems like Dr. Coppelius is David Sheppard's default role, he mused, and then he proceeded with a search on the device for possible information on murders of dancers in those cities during those months. The right side of his mouth lifted. He reached for his cell phone.

———ɷ———

Even though Fiona's body ached, the second day of rehearsal seemed to be going a little smoother than the first. The level of motivation kicked up several notches when Cynthia Montgomery strolled into the studio forty-five minutes into the rehearsal.

Fiona wasn't sure if she should feel honored, excited, or absolutely horrified. She noted that David was not only surprised, but instantly out of sorts when Cynthia arrived. Recovering quickly, he carried a chair in from the lobby for her to sit on to observe the rehearsal.

"What are you doing here, Cynthia?" David inquired.

"I was out and about and decided to see how the newest addition to the ballet was working out," she said, as she eased into the chair.

Fiona couldn't help but notice Cynthia's cane complimented her blue pantsuit. The stylish cane featured a spray of blue and purple Shasta Daisies amongst a bright white background. The cane was more like an accessory rather than a crutch. The former ballerina was the epitome of a sophisticated woman—when she wasn't dressed like a janitress.

Fiona found herself wondering what happened to the wooden cane that she saw Cynthia with in the parking garage, and she decided that it was time to ask. After all wasn't that the reason Nathan asked her to join the cast of Coppelia—to glean information?

Digging deep to find equal measures of courage and couth, Fiona said, "That is a gorgeous cane, Cynthia. I'm not sure which one I like better, the blue one I saw you with last night or this one."

"Thank you, I have quite a few. I have to use them in order to walk, so they may as well be attractive," Cynthia explained.

"I totally agree. Looks like you don't use the plain wooden one very often—the one that you had in the parking garage where I first met you on Saturday."

She hesitated. Fiona could see that she was gauging her response. "No…it's rather primitive, so I don't use that one very often. I use it when I work. No reason to take one of my good canes just to dust banisters."

"No, I guess not."

Cynthia shifted in her seat.

"Oh, by the way, here are your complimentary tickets to the Friday night show. Invite your parents or some such thing," David suggested, handing her a simple white envelope.

"Thank you."

"Now, could we please get back to rehearsal?"

"Of course," Fiona said.

After watching the rehearsal for a half-hour, Cynthia said, "I know it's difficult, Fiona, but you must trust David completely. You are a doll. Keep your body limp—draped over his arm until you are supposed to come to life. Wait for your cue as if you are asleep. You're too stiff, too anticipating of the next movement. *Relax.*"

"Oh, I don't know, Cynthia, she seems quite limp to me—like a worn out rag doll. Maybe we should re-title the ballet, Raggedy Ann," Monroe's arrogant tone bounced off the walls of the studio. Everyone's attention snapped toward the doorway where the lovely ballerina leaned against the jamb.

Fiona could almost hear the flush of agitation crawling up the back of her neck into her face. She had to bite down on her tongue not to lash out at the witch—that would accomplish nothing but more agitation. Monroe just wasn't worth the effort.

"What are you doing here, Monroe?" Cynthia hissed through clenched teeth.

"I came looking for David. Oh and you too, Fiona. I wanted to see what kind of progress you were making. Just as I suspected—nil."

"I think she's doing very well, considering how long she's been off," David defended.

"Speaking of dancers who've been off—I'm surprised to find you here, Cynthia. What's it been since you've graced a studio? Fifteen, twenty years? I would think your suggestions would be rather outdated."

Cynthia pushed up from her seat, taking several angry steps forward while pointing a warning finger at Monroe. Halting abruptly, she grabbed her cane. "I know the role of Coppelia and Swanhilda inside and out! Its classical ballet through and through. Don't you dare question my ability!"

Monroe shrugged. "The question is, will Fiona be ready by Friday's performance? From where I stand—I doubt it."

David stepped forward, taking her by the arm. He attempted to be quiet, but his words echoed through the studio. "You shouldn't be here, Monroe. We have work to do. I'll meet up with you later."

"All right, I'll go." She strutted toward the door, and then suddenly she whirled around victoriously. "FYI—they've decided to have a full cast rehearsal tomorrow, early in the evening—six o'clock."

"But that wasn't supposed to happen until Thursday," Fiona blurted out. She was taken aback by the sound of sheer panic in her own voice.

Monroe tossed her a poisonous grin. "It was, but now it's been moved up to tomorrow. Hope you don't choke, Raggedy Ann."

All the oxygen in the room seemed to be sucked out after Monroe made her exit. Fiona could see the dread in David's eyes. She could tell that he was having his misgivings about getting her ready for Friday, and had even less confidence that she would be properly prepared for the rehearsal tomorrow evening. She didn't blame him. She was having the same qualms herself.

Returning to her chair, Cynthia dug through her bag to pull out a small bottle of red wine. David growled, "*Seriously*, Cynthia?"

"Yes, *seriously*, David," she said, opening the bottle to take a quick swig. "Wake up! A deadline has been delivered by the wicked witch of the ballet. Why are you two just standing there? Let's get moving!" Cynthia called across the room, backing it up with a resounding stomp of her cane on the floor—very hard.

Seven

"I'm beginning to think that you might be right, Silja," Fiona groaned while soaking her feet in a tub of warm Epsom salts. Harriet was draped over her lap, while Fiona gently caressed her ears.

"I tried to get Evelyn to make us some tea, but it didn't work," Silja said, handing Fiona a steaming cup.

"Really? How'd you go about it?"

She demonstrated by using an English accent. "I looked up to the ceiling and said, Evelyn, could you make us some tea?"

Giggling, Fiona inquired, "And then what happened?"

"Nothing. I had to make it myself." Feigning grave disappointment, she plopped down next to Fiona on the couch. "Anyway, what do you think that I'm right about? I can't wait to hear."

"I'm beginning to think that Monroe McCarthy is deeply involved in this murder case. I mean, she blatantly showed up at the studio tonight to see David, and when she found his wife there, she didn't blink an eye. She didn't care one bit if Cynthia knew they were…involved."

"So you think she killed Alexis and whacked me over the head?"

"It's possible, I suppose. Maybe David was showing interest in Alexis. Monroe seems like someone who has to have things her way—"

"*Seems* like? Let me tell ya, honey—it's her way or the highway!"

"And maybe she sent Alexis down the highway because David had eyes for her."

Silja flipped a careless wrist. "David makes passes at everyone—including me. I know for a fact that Alexis wasn't interested in him. I think he's nothing but a dirty old man, and she thought so too."

"Doesn't matter. When a woman like Monroe is jealous, it doesn't make one bit of difference if you're innocent or not—she's going to take you out of the equation," Fiona stated. "But why? Why would a beautiful talented young woman like Monroe have an interest in David Sheppard? He's at least twice her age. I'm sure she could have just about any man she wanted."

"Some women like older men, but I think for women like Monroe it's about control. Because he's so much older and she's so pretty, he'll do anything she wants to keep her happy. For some women that's the definition of a perfect relationship." Silja blew on her tea and then took a cautious sip. "Yep, I can see that working for Monroe."

"How old do you think Cynthia is? I figured her for about his age."

"Oh no, she's much younger. I think she just looks older because of her circumstances. Cynthia is probably about fifty-five. Remember, she had just danced Coppelia the night of the accident. Most ballerinas don't perform much past the age of thirty-two or thirty-four at the oldest."

"That's true. I'd forgotten." Fiona eased her feet out of the warm water, drying them with a towel. "Well, I'd better get to bed. I'm going to be crawling on my hands and knees as it is, and tomorrow is going to be a very busy day with Alexis's funeral and all."

"I appreciate you taking off work to come with me."

"I wanted to come. Even though I didn't know her, I mean I never met her at all, I still feel a strong connection to her somehow."

"It's probably because you're so connected to the case. Alexis would appreciate everything that you're doing."

Fiona pushed up from the couch. "I have no idea how I'm going to make it through that rehearsal tomorrow evening. I can't believe they moved it up."

"It was Monroe's idea."

Fiona rolled her eyes. "Why am I not surprised?"

A somber group assembled under a canopy around Alexis Cartwright's casket Wednesday morning. Members of the ballet company filed in to the left. Fiona noticed that most of the dancers were in attendance, including David Sheppard and Cynthia. Many members of the orchestra, stage crew, ushers, and maintenance came as well. Even Monroe showed up for a fellow dancer's final goodbye. Alexis's family and personal friends congregated to the right of her casket. Detective Landry covertly squeezed in between the two groups.

The wind whipped through the canopy as the priest took his place at the head of the casket and began to read from the Bible—that's when Fiona noticed a man dressed in a black suit standing directly across from her. The priest asked them to bow their heads in prayer, but Fiona couldn't take her eyes off the man.

He looked familiar.

Where had she seen him before?

And then it hit her! He was the man who'd shared the elevator with her and Cynthia Saturday afternoon. The man who was in such a grave hurry.

Wait a minute!

He was the same man who knocked her on her butt in the middle of the crosswalk later that day!

As if he felt her eyes upon him, the man looked up. Quickly, she closed hers, and then she peeked to see if he was still looking. Fiona gently nudged Silja with her elbow. "Who is that man?" she whispered out the side of her mouth.

"What man?"

"In the black suit—across from me."

Silja chanced a quick look. "I'm not sure. He was at the funeral home, but I never had a chance to talk to him. He's a relative. I know that much."

"I've seen him before," another voice whispered. Fiona glanced to her right. It was Sara Holloway. "He came out of Alexis's dressing room shortly after I arrived on Saturday. I heard them arguing."

"Oh my God," Fiona gasped, and then remembering that she was at a funeral—several of the dancers glanced over at her. Embarrassed by her outburst, she bit her lip. Quickly, she bowed her head as if in prayer. She leaned in closer to Sara to whisper, "Did you tell Detective Landry this?"

"I—I didn't think of it. I must've forgotten all about it."

"How could you forget something like that?" Fiona hissed.

The young dancer fought back tears. "I—I dunno. I'm sorry."

As the priest continued praying, Fiona inched her way through the crowd of mourners toward Detective Landry until she was at his side. "Something I can help you with, Ms. Quinn?"

"Amen," the priest said. Quiet conversations rose from the crowd. Many stopped to hug or shake the man in the black suit's hand.

"See that man? One of the dancer's said he was in Alexis's dressing room—they were arguing. I also had an unpleasant encounter with him that day as well. I'd say he's a *'person of interest.'*

He favored her with a cockeyed smile. "Is that what you'd call him? That's Evan Cartwright—Alexis's older brother. He told me that he had visited with his sister that day, although he didn't mention an argument. That said, he seems genuinely broken up over his sister's death."

"Really? He seemed to be in a *genuinely* big hurry the day that she died. So much so that he knocked me to the ground and didn't look back."

Suddenly the detective was looking at Evan Cartwright with narrowed eyes. He said, "I'll have a conversation with the dancer and then revisit Mr. Cartwright."

—⁂—

"Look Detective, I'm sorry that I bumped into the dancer, but that doesn't prove that I killed my sister," Evan said, concisely.

"Of course it doesn't. It just proves that you're very rude when in a hurry. You knocked her to the ground and never bothered to look back."

"I'm sorry. I didn't realize."

"I'm sure that will make her feel so much better. That said, I'm more interested in an argument that another dancer claimed to overhear between you and your sister in her dressing room not long before you bumped into the woman in the crosswalk—the same woman who found your sister's body just moments afterward."

Evan planted his hands on his hips. "What are you talking about? We weren't arguing."

"I've recently discovered that your parents were killed in an automobile accident. I'm sorry. You've had quite a few losses in your life in recent years. That must be hard."

"It is hard. What are you getting at?"

"Seems Alexis inherited everything—you were cut out. Could that be the reason you were arguing with her?"

Evan let out a beleaguered sigh. "Look, I wasn't the best son, okay? And yes, maybe I was angry because they let me know it in a big way, but I wouldn't *kill* my *sister* over it. I loved Alexis. I was supposed to be at the ballet that day, but something came up—an appointment that I'd forgotten. I couldn't stay, so I stopped in to visit for a little while and wish her good luck. I was running late—for the appointment, that's why I was rushing around, but that's all there was to it."

"What was the appointment?" the detective asked.

Tapping his foot, Evan looked at the floor and then to the ceiling.

"Evan, who were you meeting with?"

"My parole officer."

"For the convenience store robbery where the clerk was shot and killed?"

Evan looked away. "Yeah, that's the one. I didn't shoot the guy. My friend got nervous and shot him. He's still in jail. Like I said, I wasn't the best person back then, but I've turned it all around. I've got a decent job. Not a high-paying or prestigious job, but it's a *good* job. I'm clean, and Alexis had a lot to do with that. Why would I kill her?"

"I hope you didn't." He turned to leave, and then whirled around to catch the door before Evan closed it. "Ya know, I like your story. I really do. But I've got a little problem—there's still several hours unaccounted for. You bumped into the woman after she'd been to your sister's performance. You were still in town. Why?"

Evan let out a frustrated sigh. "I ended up being late for the appointment after all. My parole officer wasn't happy, so he made me stick around for a drug test *and* the results." He paused. It was obvious he was measuring his words. "Look, I did go back to the theater. I wanted to see if Alexis wanted to go to lunch, but she said she just wanted to rest. So I left—that's when I prob'ly bumped into the girl in the street. Like I said, I'm sorry. I had a lot on my mind."

"Don't leave town, Evan, or you won't need a parole officer anymore. Understand?"

"I didn't kill my sister. I swear—"

"Just don't leave town."

—⁓—

Bracing for a daunting rehearsal that evening, Fiona slung her backpack over her shoulder to make her way through the parking garage. Her footsteps echoed through the large empty area. After pressing the button for the elevator, she checked her cell phone for the time, five o'clock. Not bad. She had stopped at home to let Harriet out, pulled her leotard and tights on under her skinny jeans to save time upon arriving at the rehearsal. Now she would have plenty of time to stretch—not only would it help her already sore muscles, but stretching would also relieve some of the stress crowding her chest.

The elevator door slid open and she stepped in, closing her eyes, taking deep calming breathes. The car descended to the first level. As the door slid open, Fiona almost stepped out, until she caught a glimpse of Calvin talking to someone in a car parked in one of the designated disabled parking spaces.

Calvin glanced over his shoulder to lock eyes with Fiona. Unconsciously, he stepped away from the car to reveal who was sitting inside—Cynthia Montgomery. She was wearing a floral scarf around her head and large dark sunglasses parked on her nose, but there was no mistaking that it was definitely Cynthia. Quickly, the driver's window slid up and the white Elantra backed out of the parking spot to speed out of the garage. Calvin was left behind without a place to hide. He looked guilty—of what Fiona couldn't be sure.

Tugging her knit cap over her ears, Fiona tossed him a withered smile, and then continued along her way toward the street exit and on to the theater. As she made her way, she had the creepy feeling that she was being followed. It was rush hour in Pittsburgh. The ebb and flow of the traffic was as chaotic as ever, and the sidewalks were just as hectic with hordes of people. Still the unsettling feeling hung on. She couldn't erase the image of Calvin's sheepish expression when she saw him talking with Cynthia. It was more than obvious that they didn't want to be seen together. The why of the sight kept niggling at her, while she felt compelled to glance over her shoulder, only to find strangers hurrying along to wherever, while talking on cell phones or thumbing a text message. No one was looking up—not even those in the midst of crossing the street.

A sense of relief washed over her when she reached the stage door of the Benedum. She rushed inside, tearing the cap from her head with one hand, while unzipping her coat with the other. She just wanted to tie on her pointe shoes, stretch, and get the rehearsal over with. The long hallway was empty except for the sensations that always welled within her of performers from long ago, hurrying about in preparation for a rehearsal that was sure to begin at any moment.

Dismissing the specters of the Benedum, she dropped her stuff in Silja's dressing room, dug her pointe shoes out of her backpack to make her way toward the stage. She was making her best effort not to hyperventilate. When she made the right turn out of the dressing room she noticed the maintenance room door was ajar.

While it was really none of her business what Calvin and Cynthia were talking about or if they were involved in some way, Fiona felt the need to talk with him, to put his mind at ease. Of course she was obligated to inform Detective Landry about the incident, but she didn't want him to be uncomfortable around her—she would feel most uncomfortable if he was.

Light from the small office seeped through the slight gap into the faintly lit hallway. She could see a shadow on the wall moving across the room. Tapping on the door as she pushed it open, she called, "Calvin... are you in here?" As the door fell open, Calvin jerked upward from behind his desk while trying to hide something in his hand behind the desk.

"Fiona! W-what can I help you with?"

Fiona's eyes narrowed. He was almost in a panic by her unannounced visit. What was he trying to hide? Did it have something to do with his covert conversation with Cynthia? She said, "I'm sorry that I startled you."

Whatever it was that he was attempting to conceal, he shoved it further under the desk. "No…not at all. I didn't expect you is all. Is…is there something you need?"

"I'm surprised that you're working today, being that there's no performance, only a rehearsal."

"Well, there has to be a maintenance person on site when the theater is being used. Today was an unscheduled rehearsal, so I came in instead of calling someone else—it seemed easier." He cleared his throat. "Is there something I can help you with?"

"No…I just wanted to say…that is, I…didn't want you to think that I meant to stare or make you uncomfortable in the garage just now. I mean, it's none of my business—"

"You mean when I was talking with Cynthia?" He laughed, feigning a careless demeanor. "She was just saying hello. We're old friends, Cynthia and I…it was nothing…truly."

"Oh! I didn't mean to imply…anyway, I didn't mean to stare. Have…have a nice evening."

Smiling, he nodded his reply. Fiona hurried from the room, feeling stupid. *Nice going, Fiona. Nothing like making the man feel totally awkward. What a super spy you are. Sheesh!*

Looking down at her watch, she was now behind instead of ahead. She picked up her pace down the hallway to the stage.

"I can't believe that you re-choreographed the doll dance!" Fiona heard Monroe complain as she entered the stage area to take a place at the barre that had been set up stage left.

"I felt it would be easier for her if she didn't have to be on pointe throughout the dance. I thought it would be a faster way for her to learn the part," David defended himself.

"If she can't handle the role, what is she doing here? There were plenty of other dancers who could've danced the part, David."

"Why don't you stop nagging and stretch out so we can get on with this rehearsal," Silja remarked loudly from her place on the stage where she was straddled on the floor. She shot a wink at Fiona as she rushed passed.

"I've already stretched out," Monroe snapped back.

"Well then you should work those triple pirouettes, they're looking a little weak," Silja said. Several dancers around her snickered quietly at the comment.

"Alright, alright," David put in, while holding his hands up in frustrated surrender. "Fifteen minutes and then we will begin the rehearsal—so I suggest everyone stop fooling around and get warmed up. Pleeease."

Monroe shot death daggers from her eyes at Silja as she strutted past to find an empty spot on the stage floor for stretching.

When the rehearsal finally got underway, Fiona was mesmerized by the talent that surrounded her. Oh sure, she was well aware of how beautifully they danced when she sat in the seats Saturday afternoon to watch the performance, but being amongst the dancers on the stage was an experience that stirred her soul and her memories. Even Monroe amazed her. The woman could be vindictive and nasty, but she was a magnificent dancer—there was no taking that from her.

A skeleton orchestra played during the rehearsal and only the most necessary sets were moved into position. Lighting, costumes, stage crew, and full orchestra would be brought in for the dress rehearsal tomorrow night.

Fiona sat upon her chair center stage in the set that represented Dr. Coppelius's shop staring at a pink book lying in her lap as the dancers finished their routine, and then exited stage right. The small orchestra continued to play as Silja made her appearance from stage right, while Monroe, who was dancing the part that Alexis once did, was supposed to make her entrance from stage left, except when Silja arrived at her appointed spot on stage Monroe was nowhere to be found.

From the corner of Fiona's eye she could see Silja craning her neck, looking to stage left for Monroe, yet still there was no entrance. She looked stage right at David who shrugged, rolling his eyes.

"Monroe..." Silja called over the music.

No response.

"Woohoo! Monroe..."

Still nothing.

Silja made another attempt. "Seriously, you've missed your cue!"

Noticing a problem on stage, the conductor gestured for the orchestra to stop playing.

Again Silja turned to David, who now looked very perplexed.

As brash as Monroe usually behaved, she wasn't reacting to the mistake that Silja was loudly pointing out.

They waited…

Silja threw her hands up, marched passed Fiona toward stage left to step behind the curtain.

The theater was completely silent until it was shattered by a gut-wrenching scream!

Fiona leapt from her seat to rush toward the sound of Silja's shrieks with David and several dancers on her heels. They slid to a stop to find Silja with her hand cupped over her mouth standing over Monroe's dead body!

Detective Landry circled the body of Monroe McCarthy lying on the stage floor, while the medical examiner conducted a preliminary exam. The older man wore a grimace on his lips and a pair of bifocals parked on the edge of his nose. His brow was furrowed in thought as he hovered over the corpse.

"Pretty much the same as the other girl," he noted. "Someone smacked her but good. Only this time it looks to be with more force, and possibly with a heavier object. I'll know more after a complete examination. Maybe our perp is getting angrier for whatever reason. Blunt force trauma—seems to becoming a theme around here." He stood taking in the backstage area. "Ya know, my wife drags me to the ballet 'bout three times a year."

"You don't enjoy the ballet?" Detective Landry inquired.

"Not particularly. Not that I've ever actually seen one. I sleep through most of it. Now I can tell her in all honesty that it's dangerous to our health," he explained with his mouth lifted in a sly smile. He looked up to see the paramedics waiting in the doorway with a dark body bag draped over a gurney. He waved them in to remove the body as he tore a pair of latex gloves from his hands. "This is your second victim in less than a week. Got any solid suspects, Detective?"

"Several, Ms. McCarthy was one of them, I'm afraid."

"Well, she certainly isn't anymore." With that, he scooped up his bag and made his way toward the exit.

The detective turned to find a pallid David Sheppard standing several feet away. "Should we all assume the position, Detective?" he asked, trying not to glance in the direction where the paramedics were now gathering Monroe's body.

"What position would that be, Mr. Sheppard?"

"A seat in the auditorium area like when Alexis was murdered."

"Well, I do have to interview everyone who was at the scene. Have you seen Mr. Kleppner?"

"Calvin? No, not this evening. I imagine he's at home, where I wish I was at this moment."

"Do you know anyone who would want to harm Ms. McCarthy?"

"Besides everyone? No."

"You were very close to her, weren't you, Mr. Sheppard?"

"We were...friendly, yes. But I certainly didn't do this—I was standing right there..." he pointed to stage right, "...when Monroe failed to make her entrance, and I was still standing there when Silja found her... like...*this*." He pulled a handkerchief from his pocket to wipe his watery eyes.

"Where's your wife this evening?"

David's eyes widened in indignation. "Why would you ask about Cynthia? What could she possibly have to do with this?"

"Oh, nothing of course, I was just wondering where she was this evening. I want to make sure that if she's here, she stays so she can be interviewed like the rest this time."

"Cynthia isn't working this evening. She's at the William Penn, Detective. Most likely she's drinking a glass of wine and watching a reality show."

"Cabernet?"

David studied the detective for a moment. "If you'll excuse me, I'll gather the dancers up for you." Still dabbing his eyes, he made his way quickly across the stage.

"Thank you, Mr. Sheppard," the detective called after him. "Oh! By the way…does the name Samantha Wells mean anything to you?"

David stilled. Slowly he turned to face the detective. He lowered the handkerchief from his mouth to his chest. As he closed the space between them, he replied, "Yes…she was a principal dancer at McCaw Hall in Seattle, I believe."

Detective Landry shook his head in a solemn manner. "Ya know, funny thing…if you remember correctly, she was murdered in the backstage area of McCaw Hall last year. And if I read the report right, it was during a performance of Coppelia. Weren't you playing the role of Dr. Coppelius in that show too?"

"I was…"

"Did you know Ms. Wells as well as you knew Ms. McCarthy?"

David pursed his lips, quantifying his words. "I was acquainted with Sam, yes. But I was not a suspect in that case, obviously, I mean, they let me leave Seattle, and I've not been contacted by the police since."

Detective Landry scrubbed his fingers over his jaw, thoughtfully. "I'm sure you had nothing to do with the unfortunate incident, but ya gotta admit—whatta coincidence."

"Yes…" David turned to walk away.

"Was Cynthia working for the maintenance crew at the McCaw at that time?"

David's shoulders went stiff. "I believe so, yes…"

"Again…whatta weird turn of events, wouldn't you say, Mr. Sheppard?"

"I'll gather the dancers in the auditorium, Detective Landry."

"Thanks, Mr. Sheppard. I truly appreciate all your help and cooperation."

Eight

Another murder. Another late night due to interviews with Detective Landry, and now the dark shadow hovering over Coppelia heightened the cast's anxiety about a murderer among the troupe or someone who had targeted the company or perhaps the ballet itself. Fiona wasn't sure if the word bizarre even began to describe the situation, although horrifying certainly did.

During the interview process, Fiona and Silja stepped outside for a much needed breath of air. Once again the Benedum was surrounded by police vehicles, crowds of onlookers, and news outlets in search of answers where there seemed to be none.

"How many ballerinas have to die before the Benedum does the responsible thing and closes down the show until this killer is in custody?" one news reporter asked a member of the Benedum management outside, while investigators combed through the onsite evidence inside the theater.

"That's exactly what I've come here to announce—the Benedum management along with the Pittsburgh Ballet Theater management have decided to cancel the rest of the performances of Coppelia until this investigation comes to a conclusion. We cannot begin to express our sense of loss and extreme sympathies to the family and friends of Alexis Cartwright and Monroe McCarthy."

"I guess that's it," Fiona whispered. "Guess I won't be needing those complimentary tickets that David gave me."

"I hope you're wrong. Maybe Detective Dreamboat will solve the case and the show will go on," Silja said.

"Detective *Dreamboat*?"

Silja chuckled. "I think Detective Dreamy is already taken."

"That's *Doctor Mc*-Dreamy."

"I know...I watch TV. Come on, we'd better get back inside, before they decide we're prime suspects."

"Mmmm, I think they're down one, that's for sure," Fiona took a parting glance into the crowd gathered on the sidewalk in front of the Benedum only to lock eyes with Evan Cartwright. Her chest tightened.

Silja playfully elbowed Fiona pulling her out of her funk, as they made their way into the theater. "Hey, look over there." She directed Fiona's attention across the street. "There's our friendly bodyguard, having his coffee delivered. Having him around is almost like having a stalker, but in a good way, I guess."

Sure enough, the police officer assigned to watch over them was sitting in his cruiser across the way, and the same policewoman was handing him a cup of coffee.

"I suppose," Fiona mumbled, then glanced over her shoulder. Evan was gone.

—⁘—

When they were finally excused, everyone gathered their belongings as quickly as possible to head for home. The dancers were downtrodden with worry over the uncertainty of the show and their safety. Silja held the stage door open for Fiona whose gaze fell upon the familiar police cruiser parked across the street.

Fiona nudged her friend. "Looks like our friendly bodyguard is on duty again tonight." Just then a second cruiser pulled up, and a female officer hurried to deliver a cup of coffee to the officer. The girls watched as the two officers enjoyed a quick conversation. The female officer pitched him a wink before jogging back to her cruiser. Fiona turned to Silja. "See? I think there's something other than just coffee brewing between those two."

Silja tossed her head back, laughing. "Okay, okay, you might be right. They may very well be a thing."

"Oh, it's more than a thing—its true love," Fiona insisted.

"Oh, Fiona Quinn, you're such a romantic." Silja shook her head as she continued down the sidewalk.

As the female officer's vehicle pulled from the curb the headlights glinted off something just below the short set of steps—it caught Fiona's eyes. Silja was already a good distance down the sidewalk, but Fiona stopped to take a closer look at the object that was lying next to a small dumpster that had been tipped over.

She leaned over to get a closer look.

The night shadows created a camouflage over the dumpster and the object.

She strained to see what could be peeking out from under the snow.

And then another car passed revealing its rounded head. The headlights flashed over the brass collar—of a cane! Fiona knelt down in the wet snow. She couldn't believe what she'd found—it was Cynthia's wooden cane! Her breath caught. She was certain that that was exactly what was lying in the snow. She reached down, and then just as quickly, she jerked her hands back—she knew not to touch something that could possibly be evidence from a murder. When she pushed up from the wet ground, Silja was standing over her.

"What are you doing? Are you all right? Did you fall?" Silja asked, grabbing Fiona by the arm to help her up.

"I'm fine. Look..." Fiona pointed to the cane.

"Is that..."

"I think so." Fiona dug through her backpack to retrieve her cell phone. "I'm calling Nathan...er... Detective Landry right away."

"Oh yes, call Detective Dreamboat immediately," Silja goaded.

"Is everything okay, ladies?" a man's voice inquired from behind them. They turned to find the officer who'd been assigned to watch over them. "I'm Officer Dalton, I've been sitting outside Ms. Quinn's home…"

Fiona blinked back. This was the first time she'd seen the officer close-up. He wasn't as tall as she had imagined. He was only about five foot six—maybe seven. He was broad shouldered, but much to her surprise, he had a bit of a pouch. Maybe Silja was right. Maybe she was too much of a romantic. She romanticized the officer as tall dark and handsome, when in fact he was of average height, possibly a tad overweight, and average in the looks department. She shook the thoughts from her head to focus on the moment. "Of course, Officer Dalton…I found something that I believe may be pertinent to Detective Landry's investigation." She pointed to the cane as she pressed the cell phone to her ear.

"I'll cordon off the area." He hurried back to his cruiser to retrieve a roll of crime tape from the trunk. Upon his return, he quickly created a ten foot barrier around the dumpster and the cane.

"Detective Landry…its Fiona, I think you'd better come back to the Benedum right away. I think I found Cynthia Montgomery's missing cane."

—◈—

Silja and Fiona sat in the warmth of Officer Dalton's cruiser while Detective Landry and a crime scene investigator examined the wooden cane. Fiona noticed that Silja nervously clutched her cell phone. She asked, "Still nothing from your husband?"

Silja let out a long careworn sigh. "No. I'm really starting to worry—it's been over a week. I suppose I could contact Clark Rhodes, he's the man who oversees the ops and is in constant contact with the guys while they're gone, but Grant doesn't like me to do that."

"I don't think I could wait. I'd be calling him."

Silja's lips curled. "Clark is a nice guy. Good looking too. I'd introduce you to him if it weren't for Detective Dreamboat."

Fiona snorted in reply. Just then the car door opened and Detective Landry scooted into the front seat. He twisted his body to talk to the girls through the caging stationed between the front seats and the back.

His nose and cheeks were kissed with a rosy chill. He flashed his 1000-megawatt smile. "Good job spotting the cane, Ms. Quinn. We can't be absolutely sure that it belongs to Ms. Montgomery, but it's a good guess. The bad news is that it's been wiped clean. The CSI did a quick onsite test—there's no blood residue or hair stuck to it or even so much as a fingerprint. And they did a thorough job too. They wiped it down with alcohol."

"That's too bad," Fiona said.

"Well sorta, it is, yes. But I've got one more favor to ask of you Fio—er…Ms. Quinn. Are you up for one more police adventure?"

Silja raised an eyebrow at Fiona, who shrugged. "Sure…why not? What do you want me to do now?"

"I want you to help me trap a murderer," Detective Landry said.

"How?"

He winked. "I've got a plan."

Nine

Shifting from one foot to the other, Fiona waited at the door. She was aware that it would probably take Cynthia a little longer to answer. She found it most interesting that when one has a cane in their hand the automatic reaction is to lean upon it, and thusly, she found herself doing so.

The knob jiggled and then the door jerked open. At first Cynthia seemed a little taken aback by who she found standing on the other side, but soon her shoulders relaxed, and she favored Fiona with a pleasant smile.

"Fiona, how nice of you to drop by," she said, switching the blue cane from her right hand to her left. It was the same chic blue cane she'd had the night Fiona first came to the hotel to meet her.

"I hope I'm not interrupting anything." Trying to keep her hands from shaking, she held up the wooden cane. "I found your cane and…and I thought I'd drop by to give it to you."

Cynthia's eyes flicked to the cane in Fiona's hand. Recognition flooding her expression, her eyebrows raised, while she sucked in a short breath, and then seemingly to find her words, she managed, "My work cane…where did you find it?" Setting the blue cane aside, she took the cane from Fiona's hand.

Fiona's breath caught. She'd rehearsed the answer to this question with Nathan. After all, there was no doubt that Cynthia was going to ask where she'd found it. Yet the prepared response had escaped her. Her throat felt suddenly dry.

Think Fiona, think. You're blowing it.

"Um…I found it lying backstage…right there backstage, behind the curtain, in plain view. You know how that goes…you look and look and look for something and you find it where you never bothered to look—right out in the open. I've learned to stop looking for things I've misplaced. If I stop looking, it usually turns up on its own. Well, not on its own, that would be impossible, but I usually do find what I'm looking for if I just relax and stop searching—" She cleared her throat. "That's how it is for me anyway. I'm always misplacing things."

"Well…how nice of you to take time out of your busy schedule to bring it by. Won't you come in for a cup of tea or a glass of wine?" Cynthia set the wooden cane against the wall, taking up the blue cane.

Fiona's insides were shaking so hard that she feared she may pee herself. She feigned a confident smile and stepped into the room. "Tea would be nice, thank you."

"Oh, good." Cynthia peered down the hallway and then closed the door gently. "I was most impressed with your dancing the other day during rehearsal. I'd really like to hear why you didn't pursue a career in dance. Please, have a seat, my dear."

Fiona slowly sank into the chair near the window. Beads of sweat were forming on her brow. She unbuttoned her coat. "Oh…well…I had a skiing accident that kind of ruined my aspirations of becoming a dancer."

"How terrible. Sort of like me—as you know, an accident ended my career," Cynthia put in as she poured water into a cup, plopping a teabag roughly into the water with a splash. She placed the cup in the microwave behind the bar, setting the timer.

"Well, mine wasn't nearly as serious as your accident. I mean, mine wasn't life changing, like yours. Well, it was life changing in that I didn't become a dancer, but it didn't change the way I lived my life like yours did. Mine was a simple skiing accident—at Seven Springs. I took a bad fall and ripped my meniscus in my right knee."

"And that was enough to stop you from becoming a dancer?"

"Unfortunately, it was." Fiona took in a braced breath. "You know…I'm so glad I stopped by. I feel a special connection to you, Cynthia. If you don't mind my saying."

"How sweet. I'm so glad. I think you're a special young lady too. I think it takes a lot of moxie to take part in a major ballet production after such a long absence. You should be proud."

"Thank you for that." The buzzer on the microwave went off, causing Fiona to flinch. She took in a breath, trying to muster the courage she needed to continue. "I had an interesting conversation with Calvin Kleppner earlier today."

"Calvin is a good friend of mine. He's such a darling man," Cynthia said.

"Yes…I saw you talking with him in the parking garage." Cynthia tensed at the comment. Fiona continued, "He…he told me a secret."

Taking the cup from the microwave, Cynthia stilled. "Really…a secret? What did he tell you?"

"He said that he was the one who hit you all those years ago."

Cynthia whirled around, dropping the cup on the floor. "What? Why would he tell you such a terrible thing?"

"I'm not sure. Maybe he felt the need to get it off his chest."

As if she was completely unaware that she'd broken the cup, Cynthia strode toward Fiona, stabbing her cane against the floor with every stride. "But…but he barely knows you."

Stiffening in her seat, Fiona supplied, "Sometimes it's easier to tell, or to unload, your burden on a stranger. I don't know why—"

"What else did he say? Tell me!"

Nathan had warned her that Cynthia may become aggressive so she tried to keep her cool. She took in another steadying breath before she continued with the subterfuge. "He said that you stepped out from between two vehicles, he didn't want to leave you there, but he panicked and took off. He said that he has carried that guilt all these years because he admired you so much, and he felt so sorry for destroying your career."

Her body rigid, Cynthia eased down onto the edge of the bed. "I can't believe he told you this."

"Did you know? I mean...did you suspect that he was the one?"

Cynthia's gaze snapped to meet Fiona's for a moment, then dropped to the floor. Fiona could see in the woman's eyes that she was measuring her words and her actions. Cynthia lifted her right shoulder. "Thank you for bringing the cane to me, Fiona. But if you don't mind, I'd like to be alone. I need to think about what you've told me."

"I understand." Fiona made her way to the door, stopping before she reached for the knob. "I just hope...well, never mind—"

"What? What were you going to say?"

"The murders...I'm worried that Calvin might be involved."

Cynthia took in a tiny involuntary gasp. She pushed up from the bed. "What do you mean?"

"I'm not sure, is it possible that he killed Alexis and Monroe?"

"W-why would you think that?"

"He told me that he loved you, and that no one could dance the role of Swanhilda or Coppelia like you could. He said that Alexis and Monroe were poor replacements for the *great* Cynthia Montgomery, and Silja...well he wasn't very impressed with her either." She cleared her throat. "Someone tried to kill her the other night, too. She was hit over the head in the parking garage, only the person got away before finishing her off. Did you know about that?"

"I did, but I doubt very much that our sweet Calvin had anything to do with that or the murders of Alexis and Monroe. He doesn't have a wicked bone in his body. I think your imagination is running away with you. I mean, how does any of that connect Calvin to the murders?"

Fiona inched her way toward Cynthia. She was hitting a nerve so she needed to press on. "Don't you find it the least bit suspicious that he named all three dancers during our conversation? The two who were killed, Alexis and Monroe, and the one who got away, Silja. These are the women who are dancing your part, while you work as a janitress. I think Calvin can't bear the sight. I think he—"

"You're forgetting that you also are playing a role that I once danced, and yet no one has made an attempt on your life. Why you just told me that you and Calvin had an intimate conversation. He probably had every opportunity to harm you then, but he didn't. Quite frankly, I don't want to talk about this anymore, Fiona. And I think you should keep your suspicions to yourself," Cynthia insisted as she made her way to the door.

"Why, Cynthia? Am I on to something? Do you think he's involved? Are *you* involved?"

Cynthia's grip was so taut on the cane that her knuckles had turned white. "I think you should go, *now!*"

"If you know something, Cynthia, you should speak up now, before anymore dancers are harmed or killed—"

"I know that I'm done with this conversation, and I want you to leave." Cynthia pulled the door open.

Fiona's heart sank.

She'd failed.

Impatience quickly took hold, and Cynthia hitched her chin in the direction of the hallway. "Now, Fiona, I want you to leave now. And as I said, you'd best keep those ridiculous thoughts to yourself."

Fiona stepped into the hallway, the door slamming after her. She made her way to the elevator. When the door opened, she stepped inside the empty car and pressed the lobby button. Defeat weighed down on her shoulders as she crossed her arms over her chest and then leaned against the wall.

Certain that she was completely alone, she whispered into her earpiece, "She didn't take the bait. She didn't tell me anything that you wanted to hear. At least I don't think she did."

"It ain't over 'til the fa—oh, there's no fat lady in ballet, is there?"

Fiona giggled. "No, Nathan, there isn't, but I get what you're saying."

"You did a fine job, Fiona. You accomplished exactly what we needed. She's shook up, and now is a good time for a visit from yours truly. A police officer is waiting for you outside the hotel. He's dressed in a really cheesy brown suit with a yellow tie—"

"Hey! This is the best suit I own, and my wife bought me this tie last Christmas." A man's voice broke through the connection along with snide comments from other officers on the surveillance crew parked outside the William Penn.

"*Ouch*, well, the tie isn't so bad, but you gotta get a better suit, man," the detective told him. "Anyway, Fiona, the officer's name is Wyatt and he's pretending to smoke a cigarette right outside the main entrance. He'll remove all the wires and take you home. I'll catch up with you later…um…if that's okay."

No one could see her. It was perfectly safe to smile as big as she desired, dance in a small circle, while victoriously pumping both fists in the air—so she did. After the *happy dance* ritual, she pulled herself together enough to calmly reply, "I'll brew some coffee."

"Sounds good. Hey, David Sheppard just entered the building—wait…okay, they said he got on the other elevator. You're clear. Gotta go, thanks Fiona."

You're very welcome, Detective Dreamboat. Fiona hoped that no one on the other end of the earpiece heard the tiny giggle that escaped.

———ɯ———

Detective Landry brushed off the chill from his quick walk to the hotel from the surveillance van. As the elevator made its way upward, he pressed his cold hands into the pockets of his coat. His fingers ran into a clump of tiny foil squares. The right side of his mouth lifted when he realized that he had a pocketful of bite size Snickers bars from who knew when.

"Prob'ly stale," he muttered as the elevator doors slid open. He shoved them back into his pocket as he made his way down the hallway to David Sheppard and Cynthia Montgomery's suite.

Cynthia's expression was one of composed trepidation when she opened the door to find the detective standing on the other side. With the pointer finger of the hand holding a glass of wine she swept an errant strand of hair from her brow, painting on a pleasant expression. "Detective Landry, how nice to see you again."

The detective heard David groan loudly from somewhere inside the suite. With his hands pressed deep in the pockets of his coat, Detective Landry said, "It sure is chilly outside. You should be glad you don't have to be out in it."

"Indeed, what brings you by, Detective?" she inquired.

"You know, a detective's paperwork is never done. I've come across some things in an old file that need some attention and my captain insisted that I see to it right away. You know how bosses can be, very…bossy."

Bringing the wine glass to her chest, she asked, "What old file are you talking about?"

"Do you mind if I come in? I don't like to discuss police business in the hallway—too many nebby-noses in a hotel."

"Oh…of course…um…come in, Detective," she said, stepping aside to allow him entry. Several drops of the wine sloshed over the glass falling to the carpet. "Oopsie! I'm always dripping, I'm afraid."

Looking at the many tiny red stains over the carpeting in the room, Detective Landry agreed. "Yes, I noticed. In fact you left a drop of wine in your husband's Mercedes, and I noticed a drop or two of red wine on the carpet in Calvin Kleppner's office when I spoke with him." He looked up to find David scowling at him from the mini bar. "Hi, Mr. Sheppard, glad to see you're feeling better."

"Really? When wasn't I feeling well, Detective?" David asked through clenched teeth as he gingerly threw several pieces of broken china into the waste can.

"At the theater after Monroe's murder, I guess it was hard because the two of you were so close. I understand, believe me. I suppose you must've been pretty shook up after Samantha Wells' death, too."

"I told you that I had *nothing* to do with that."

"Didja break something?"

"Cynthia dropped a cup of tea." David snatched a martini glass from the bar.

Detective Landry's lips curled as he pulled a handful of the tiny Snickers bars from the pocket of his coat. "Well, I'll be. Ya never know what you'll find in a coat that you haven't worn in a while." He held the candy out toward Cynthia. "Would you like a Snickers? They're bite size. Just right for a quick snack—sugar rush. Sometimes I need one with the long hours I keep." He fumbled to unwrap one.

"Cynthia shouldn't have chocolate. It brings on her headaches," David groused.

"Ooh...yeah, my sister avoids chocolate for the same reason. Sure am glad I don't have that problem," he said, tossing the Snickers into his mouth. Shrugging, he stuffed the candy back into his pocket. Around a mouthful of chocolate, he continued, "Ya know, it's a funny thing..."

he opened his coat to dig in the inside pocket, producing a folded and wrinkled file jacket. He opened the file and with furrowed brows, he studied it for a moment. Cynthia took a long sip of her wine. Slowly he dragged his gaze to meet hers. "It says right here, that the homicide detective that worked the Samantha Wells murder case...Fred...Fred Kearns, do you remember him?"

"Sorry, I'm afraid I don't," Cynthia replied.

"Anyway, it says here in the file that he found drops of wine here and there during the investigation into Samantha Wells death, including in her dressing room, and he mentions that the janitress' that worked at the McCaw Hall complained of finding drops of wine in their lunch room. You were working as a janitress at the time, weren't you, Ms. Montgomery?"

Cynthia narrowed her eyes. "I was."

"The girls weren't too happy about the stains. Seems they had a devil of a time getting those stains out of the carpet. Now, here's where it gets really funky—upon testing the wine, it turned out to be cabernet. Isn't that the kind of wine we lifted off the mat in your Mercedes, Mr. Sheppard?"

David stopped mixing his martini. His jaw clenched.

Detective Landry unwrapped another piece of candy. The foil crinkled loudly.

Cynthia swirled the wine around and around in her glass, while studying the liquid legs that slowly slid down the curve of the glass, as if she had grown bored with the conversation. "As a matter of fact, it's what I'm drinking right now."

"Lots of people drink cab, Detective. It proves nothing, nothing at all," David said.

"You're absolutely right, Mr. Sheppard." He tossed another Snickers into his mouth. "Except I got to thinking, why would there be a spot of cabernet on Mr. Kleppner's office carpet unless he and Ms. Montgomery were in there together? If you remember, you yourself told me that she liked to borrow those small bottles of wine they sell at the theater."

Letting out a beleaguered sigh, David scrubbed his forehead with his fingers.

Detective Landry continued, "Naturally, my curiosity got the best of me. My mom always told me I should become a detective because of my natural inquisitiveness. Anyway, during my conversation with Mr. Kleppner, he said something that got me to thinking about that night you were hit by the car."

Cynthia sat down on the closest bed. "What could he have possibly said to make you think about that?"

"Well, I distinctly remember how attentive Mr. Kleppner was to you every time I saw you together at the theater the day of the murder. In fact, during one of my conversations with him, he told me how badly he felt about your accident, and how whoever was responsible was prob'ly afraid of the repercussions for hitting a pedestrian and that's why they fled the scene. Never once did he condemn the person who'd hit you and ended your career. Instead he made excuses for the individual. He showed compassion for them. I found that to be very strange."

"Calvin is a very compassionate soul," Cynthia put in.

"That's a whole lot of sympathy for someone who'd destroyed an angel from Heaven—a gift from God, is the way I believe he put it when he spoke of you. Calvin was a fan, Ms. Montgomery—a *big* fan. Furthermore, I had the DMV check on vehicles that Mr. Kleppner owned during that time period, and guess what I found?"

"I have no doubt that you're going to tell us," David moaned.

"A blue 1993 Chevy Impala." He paused to take in David and Cynthia's baffled expressions. "True, they never found the vehicle that hit you, but one of the women who witnessed the accident insisted that the car was blue and that it was a Chevy. Here's my theory: I believe he'd do anything for you, including kill the women who were dancing the roles that you once danced and were entertaining your husband at the same time."

David rushed around the bar toward the detective. "So you're saying that you've caught the murderer? You're saying that Calvin was clubbing these poor women to death on behalf of my Cynthia?"

Detective Landry put his hand up in a halting manner. "Almost, but not quite. Somehow Ms. Montgomery figured out that Calvin was the one, didn't you, Cynthia?"

"The one who killed those girls? I had no idea—"

"You knew he was the one who hit you all those years ago on Seventh Street in front of the Benedum, although at the time it was called the Stanley. Isn't that right?"

Slowly, she made her way to the bar and took a seat on one of the stools. She swirled the deep red wine around inside the glass. "Calvin confessed that he was the one, yes. He was looking for my forgiveness."

"And you were willing to give it to him, but at a price. Isn't that right?"

"What is he saying, Cynthia? Calvin was the one who ran you over? Why didn't you tell me? Why didn't you tell the police?" David asked, breathless.

"She had bigger ideas," Detective Landry said. "She'd killed Samantha Wells and Alexis Cartwright, but she really wanted Monroe McCarthy out of the way, and that's where Calvin came in. Isn't that right, Ms. Montgomery?"

Still she sat motionless, quietly continuing to swirl the liquid inside the walls of the curved glass. Red faced, David stared at her anticipating her response. Confounded by her silence, he looked at the detective, and then back at Cynthia. "Say something, Cynthia!

He can't be right. You would never do something so horrible!"

Without warning, Cynthia turned on the stool, pitching the glass to the floor. The glass shattered. The wine seeped quickly across and into the fibers of the carpeting. "*Really*, David? *Really*? What evidence does he have? A few stains in the carpet? A list of cars that Calvin once owned that may or may not have been involved in my accident all those years ago? Really?" She let out a haughty laugh. "It was cabernet, was it? Is Detective Landry absolutely sure that none of the janitress' at the McCaw didn't steal the little bottles and drink cab? Or was it just me? So I'm the only one who's ever drank or spilled a little cab on the floor. That's your evidence, Detective Landry? How perfectly ridiculous."

"If you don't mind my sayin'—I don't think so. The day I spoke with Mr. Kleppner in his office I retrieved a perfectly good half-empty bottle of alcohol, and an empty bottle of wine from his waste bin. You know, one of those little five ounce bottles from the theater bar—cabernet. Anyway, just got it back from the lab, your prints were found on the wine bottle."

"Are…are you allowed to just take things from the waste bin like that?" Cynthia stammered. "I mean, don't you need a *warrant* for that?"

The detective waved a careless hand. "Naw…it was abandoned and in plain sight. If it had been in Mr.

Kleppner's house I couldn't have claimed it, but it was at his place of employment. I asked the Benedum management if I could have it, and well, they didn't care. Mind telling me what you and Mr. Kleppner were discussing when you were in his office? Forgiveness and how he could earn it, perhaps?"

"I don't have to tell you a thing, Detective Landry. Everything you have is circumstantial. You can't prove a thing—not a thing."

"You're right, of course. I mean, we can't even prove that the Chevy was involved in your accident, because we have no one to identify the vehicle—not to mention that we don't have the vehicle either. But, guess what? Much to my disappointment, your cane had been completely wiped clean—with alcohol. So, we tested the remaining alcohol in the bottle—the one I retrieved from the waste can in Calvin's office, and the residue we found on the cane—they matched, the alcohol was from the same batch that was in the bottle. Let me tell you what else we have..." He made his way to the wooden cane left leaning against the wall. Picking it up, he made a big show of examining the cane with narrowed eyes under the hook of the handle. He could see Cynthia snatch another glass and pour more cabernet, as he walked the cane over to David. "Yeah, yeah, see *ri-i-i-i-ght* here..." He pointed to a small area under the hook, and right above the brass collar.

Cynthia fidgeted in her seat, biting her lip, craning her neck to see what the detective was showing to her husband.

David bent down to examine the spot where the detective was pointing. He squinted and strained to see what he was trying to show him. "I don't see what you're pointing at, Detective."

"I'm sure you don't. It's too small. It's a partial stained fingerprint. Guess what the stain is—cabernet. If you look, the wood is slightly cracked as well."

"I don't see a crack either," David said.

"It's very, very tiny—"

"Let me see that stupid cane!" Cynthia cried out, while jerking from her seat. She snatched the cane from Detective Landry's hand. "Where? Where is the crack and the cabernet stain?"

Detective Landry could sense her unsteady emotions. The wine was now in the driver's seat of her actions. He pointed to the area that he'd been directing David to. She looked and examined and studied the part until she was rife with frustration. As quick as a ninja she swung the cane at the detective cracking him across the head, knocking him to the floor!

"Cynthia!" David shrieked, too shocked to move.

Detective Landry was dazed. The room was moving around and up and down. He shook his head, trying to gather his wherewithal, when through blurred vision he saw Cynthia raise the cane over her head to strike him again. The detective rolled to the left to escape the blow, while intertwining his legs around her ankles to bring her crashing to the floor with a hard thud.

The former ballerina may have been older, and she may have been disabled, but she managed to hold onto the cane, whipping it down over his stomach. The detective let out a grunt, except this time he grabbed hold of the cane yanking it from her grasp, while David hooked his arms under her shoulders to haul her kicking and screaming away from the detective.

"Cynthia! Stop!" David yelled, but she kicked and screamed and struggled all the more.

Detective Landry used the cane to pull himself from the floor just as the door burst open. Two officers with guns drawn hurried into the room. "You okay, Landry?" one officer asked.

Rubbing his head as he tried to focus, the detective said, "I think so. What made you guys come up?"

The officer snorted. "You must'a bumped your radio. We heard the struggle. Didn't want you to get too beat up by an older woman, so we came to help you out."

"She took me by surprise." The detective scowled at the officer and the thumping in his head, as he strode in an unsteady manner toward Cynthia. "You pack one heck of a punch, Ms. Montgomery. You're under arrest for assaulting a police officer."

"You men are all alike." She yanked her arms from David's hold. "I could never depend on you!"

"How can you say that, Cynthia? All these years I've stuck by you. I took care of you!"

"Ha! You did nothing but take care of yourself! I couldn't depend on Calvin either! I told him that I could never forgive him and that I would report him to the police for hitting me all those years ago if he failed with Monroe. Well, he took care of business when his own skin was on the line! But then the idiot told Fiona Quinn! I guess he felt the need to unburden himself once again! No one cared about me! No one cared about my pain! No one cared about all my years of suffering!"

She stopped. She bit her lip. She'd just confessed to everything. There was no taking it back.

Her eyes flicked around the room—to David, to Detective Landry, to the two police officers, and back to David. "I think I need a drink," she whispered.

"I think you've had quite enough," David said low and terse.

"Do you know the whereabouts of Mr. Kleppner, Ms. Montgomery?" Detective Landry asked.

Turning away, while lifting her chin to a haughty level, Cynthia remained silent.

Detective Landry nodded at one of the officers and he stepped forward, pulling a set of handcuffs from his utility belt. "Cynthia Montgomery you are under arrest for the murder of Monroe McCarthy and Alexis

Cartwright—" the officer began while escorting her toward the door, except Cynthia pulled to a halt before they made it to the hall.

"Wait! Wait just one moment! You are wrong! I had nothing against Alexis. She was a lovely dancer, and she wasn't a bit interested in my husband. I think she saw him for what he is—a dirty old man! I had nothing to do with that murder!"

Detective Landry's brows fell into a severe V. He tilted his head to one side as the former ballerina attempted to lie about the number of murders she'd participated in.

Cynthia added, "That said, I suppose it would be wise to inform you that Calvin is busy…tying up a loose end. A loose end that *he* created!" With that she urged the officer forward.

Detective Landry stared at the empty doorway momentarily, deciphering what Cynthia had just alluded to. Feverishly, he dug through his pockets hunting for his cell phone only to find a handful of Snickers in the right pockets. He tossed them to the floor, to begin rifling through the left. Empty. Finally he found the phone in his hip pocket. He dialed Fiona's phone.

It rang, and rang, and rang, and then he dialed Wyatt's phone only to listen to it ring and ring.

Ten

When Wyatt pulled his unmarked SUV up to Fiona's house, the police cruiser that had been sitting there keeping watch for the past week wasn't in its assigned spot.

"Isn't Officer Dalton supposed to be watching the house?" Wyatt asked.

Fiona pulled her cell phone from her backpack. The light illuminated her face as she searched for a text from Silja. Sure enough, the text was there...

> *I'm going to the coffee shop with the dancers for a little while to chill.*
> *Be home soon. Hope everything went okay. All details when I get back!*

"It's okay, Silja and Officer Dalton should be here any moment. I'll be fine."

Wyatt got out of the vehicle to open the door for her. "I'll walk you into the house and do a quick walk through to make sure it's secure."

"It's really not necessary—"

"Don't argue. I'm coming in," he said as they made their way up the walk toward the porch.

Once again the porch light was shining, yet Fiona hadn't left it on. Actually, she was quite used to the light being on when she would return home late in the evening, except with all this murder business the past week she appreciated it more. Having Evelyn around was like having her own little guardian angel. The perks consisted of nothing more than the illuminated porch light or the coffee brewing in the morning, but it was nice to know someone was there, watching over her. Yeah...with her mom and dad in Florida, it was comforting to know that she was in good hands. Her heart swelled with the love of family and home. As she pushed the key into the lock, they could hear fussing from inside, Harriet—another family member whom she loved dearly.

"You've got a little security system, have you?" Wyatt said with a chuckle in his voice.

"She makes a lot of noise, but I don't think she'd be much help in a bad situation," Fiona said.

"Ya never know. I've heard that little dogs can be fiercer than a big one."

She pushed the door open. "That's yet to be proven in Harriet's case."

The moment Wyatt stepped into the house he went into "police" mode. Oh sure, he glanced down and smiled at the little Maltese yipping at him from the confines of her crate, but then he drew his gun, gestured for Fiona to wait at the door, and stealthily made his way upstairs. A few minutes later, he returned to the foyer to continue his scrutiny throughout the rest of the house.

Confident that he wouldn't find anything or anyone to speak of, Fiona set her backpack on the floor next to the door. She took off her coat, gloves, and her knit cap. Stuffing the gloves into the cap, she then shoved the small bundle into the sleeve of the coat. She hung the coat on a hook, and then retrieved a thankful Harriet from her crate. She cuddled the little bundle of fluff in her arms while waiting for the officer to search the house for bad guys.

Several minutes later, Wyatt emerged from the basement, holstering his weapon and wearing a grimace on his face. "You really should have that basement door replaced. One good kick and an intruder would be in like Flynn. But it was a good idea to put the little dresser in front of it. I don't think it would hold anyone back who really wanted in, but it might slow them down."

Fiona cocked her head to one side. "Dresser in front the door? I didn't—"

"Yeah, the old dresser. About four drawers, pretty beat up."

"Oh…yeah, *that* dresser. *In like Flynn*? I haven't heard that expression in forever," Fiona said in an attempt to change the subject.

He winced. "My mother-in-law uses it. I can't believe I just did. Let's try to forget I said it. I should stay until Officer Dalton arrives."

"It's forgotten, but it's really not necessary that you stay. You've checked out the house—it's clear of all evil. Silja and Officer Dalton should be here soon. I'll be fine."

"Are you sure? I don't want to get in trouble with Landry—" Instantly he sucked in his lips to a thin straight line. He'd made a slip—it was obvious that he shouldn't have said what just came out of his mouth.

Fiona smiled her understanding. At the same time her heart skipped several beats. "Tell Detective Landry I insisted that the coast was clear."

Trying to act as casual as possible, he patted Harriet on the head. "Have a nice evening, Ms. Quinn."

"Thank you, Wyatt, oh and by the way, I don't think the suit is all that bad."

Pitching her a svelte smile, Wyatt insisted, "Make sure you lock the door behind me."

"I will."

"I'm gonna stand here until you do."

"Okay." With that, she closed the door, slid the lock into position, and listened for his footsteps across the porch and down the short set of steps. She watched through the beveled glass as the SUV's headlights drifted down Oxford Street. "Hmmm, a dresser in front of the basement door. Maybe we should go downstairs and have a little look at what Grandma Evelyn has been up to."

She flipped on the light and made her way down the rickety wooden stairs, past the old upright piano

with an inch of dust lying over it, and across the basement to indeed find the old dresser that her neighbor
had helped her carry down. It was designated to go out
on the next "big trash" pickup day. Now it was sitting
against the door, just as Wyatt said it was.

She smiled at the sight. Her grandma guardian angel was at it again, making sure she was safe,
although as Wyatt pointed out, she wasn't so sure that
the dresser would really make that big of a difference,
but it warmed her heart that Evelyn had made a val-
iant effort. God bless her.

"Well, Harriet, I'd better make some coffee. Nathan
said he'd come over after he talked with Cynthia."

She set the dog's feet to the cement floor and with
a nip in her step, Fiona made her way back upstairs to
the kitchen when all the lights went out. She stilled,
listening. Only the patter of Harriet's paws against the
wood floor made any sound. Had the electric gone
out? There was no wind to speak of outside. No snow-
storm bearing down on the Pittsburgh area. Closing the
basement door, she stretched her neck to look out the
kitchen window at the end of the hall. The homes in the
short distance all had lights shining in their windows.
Hmmm...

Continuing toward the kitchen, she ran her hands
along the wall in search of the light switch. Her fingers found the switch—it was down, as if someone had
turned the light off. She flipped it on to flood the foyer

with light once more, and then she stepped into the kitchen, turning that light on as well. When she was half way across the room the lights went dark again.

"Okay, what's this all about?" she murmured to herself, trying not to allow paranoia to crowd her mind. She marched back to the wall and flipped the light on again, only to have the switch automatically snap to the off position. Fiona let out a beleaguered breath. "Seriously?" She shrugged. "Okay Grandma Ev, guess I'm making the coffee in the dark."

Harriet followed her around the kitchen as she retrieved the coffee from the fridge—where the inside light was working perfectly. Then she got the coffee filters from the pantry and had no problem running a pot full of water from the faucet for the coffee machine's reservoir. Hmmm, the electric was working just fine, so why were the switches acting so peculiarly? Then again, was it the switches or was Evelyn playing some sort of a game?

She turned the coffee maker on—and it worked just fine.

Again she attempted to turn the lights on, and again the light switches instantly turned off.

Fiona rapped her fingernails on the counter in contemplation. *What gives?* With no recourse to argue with the electricity or the ghost who'd suddenly turned stubborn, she sat down at the small kitchenette to wait for the coffee to brew.

Ten minutes later the house remained dark, but the coffee was ready. She poured a cup and with only the glimmer from the streetlights filtering through the curtains. Fiona settled on the couch with her mug in hand, and Harriet jumped up next to her for a cuddle. A gentle snow had begun to fall. Fiona could see the flakes dancing under the light of the streetlamp. *Ahhh, how peaceful.* She wondered how things were going on Nathan's end. Nathan…now there was a peaceful thought indeed. Even with all the bad things happening she liked the thoughts of Nathan.

What would it be like to be involved with a homicide detective?

That was silly…he was just coming over for coffee—or to ask more questions about Monroe's murder.

On the other hand…Wyatt had made that slip-up.

Had Nathan told Wyatt he was interested in her?

A loud *creak* sounded from somewhere in the house. From the basement? Or just Evelyn banging around? The creak turned into a rumble and slide. Fiona hesitated, mid-sip from her mug. That definitely came from the basement. Okay…maybe that was actually the furnace.

Harriet's ears twitched while she fidgeted to get comfortable on the throw pillows. Fiona cocked her head to listen more closely. *Click*…it sounded nearby—the hallway? Her body tensed. Ever so slowly, she set her cup on the end table, leaning forward to listen again. Harriet's snoring kicked in making it almost impossible to hear anything at all. Gently, she shook the little dog. Harriet tossed her an annoyed look, and then plopped her head against the pillows to resume her nap.

The floor in the hallway creaked. Okay, it was official. Someone was in the house. Fiona was sure of it. Evelyn's attempt to block the door was noble, but not quite enough. Silja and Wyatt were right—she should've had the basement door fixed, long ago.

Too late.

Eleven

Now Fiona understood why the house was draped in darkness—Evelyn knew someone was sneaking around the house—waiting to enter. Most people would find that deduction ridiculous. Most people would call an electrician—not in this house. Fiona wasn't going to question her ghostly grandmother's method of security.

Fiona eased from the couch to make her way into the dining room. The silhouette of a man slipped from the kitchen into the hallway. Now with a wall between them, she couldn't see where he was or where he was going. If she could get to her backpack she could get to her cell phone.

The house was silent.

Where had he gone?

She listened for footsteps on the stairs...nothing.

Taking a chance, she peeked around the corner—a slight glow from the moon through the beveled glass on the door lent a bit of light. No one appeared to be in the hallway. On a braced breath, she stepped into the hallway and, on tiptoes, began to inch her way toward the foyer where her backpack lay next to the door. Get the backpack—get out the door—plan in place. Good. It was only fifteen feet or so to the front door, yet it seemed like a mile. She kept her body tucked against the wall as she crept slowly toward her goal—the backpack and the door.

Finally she'd made it to the end of the hall. Her right shoulder now at the arch that led from the foyer into the living room. The area from the arch to the door was a wide open space—easily seen and accessible from the living room. She made a quick move to the stairs, sitting on the bottom step. Peering through the first and second banister, she made sure no one was approaching from the living room. Leaning forward, she reached for the backpack, but it was just out of her reach. She stretched her fingers—not happening.

Harriet growled—low and mean, as mean as an eight pound cutie pie can growl anyway. Oh no! Wait! In her caution to be as quiet as possible, she'd left Harriet sleeping on the couch! Hopefully, when she made her escape, Harriet would make a dash for the door. She usually did, so it was a good chance that she would now.

Fiona let out the breath she'd been holding. *No time or options left. Just make a quick move—grab the backpack and run out the door, and leave it open for Harriet to follow.* In one sweeping movement, she pushed from the step to grab the backpack. Her cell phone started to ring from inside the bag.

It rang and rang and rang.

Harriet let out a bark. Fiona had her left hand on the backpack and her right on the doorknob when someone grabbed her by the arm, jerking her away from the door and slamming her against the wall!

Now Harriet was on her feet on top of the throw pillows growling and snarling and barking.

After being dazed for a moment, Fiona opened her eyes to find herself face to face with Calvin Kleppner. She could feel his heavy panicked breaths brushing over her face.

"Calvin!"

At this point, Harriet bravely leapt from the couch to grab the hem of Calvin's pants in her teeth, snarling and growling, while shaking her head feverishly to and fro. He shook his foot in an attempt to release his pants from the dog's grip to no avail.

"Your dog won't let go!"

"I've heard that little dogs can be fiercer than big ones. So, kudos for Harriet."

"Do you mind if I give her a little kick?"

"I certainly do!"

Calvin let out a frustrated sigh. "I'm sorry, Fiona, but you were just getting too close. Why didn't you stay away? Why didn't you just stay out of it? I like you, I really do, but—"

"What? What are you talking about?" Her eyes widened. She didn't want to believe it. "Oh my God!

You really did kill Alexis…and Monroe! Why? Why would you do such a thing?"

Keeping a strong hold on her arm, Calvin took a small step back. "No! I didn't kill Alexis! And I didn't want to kill Monroe. I didn't want to, really I didn't, but she made me do it. I'm a good person, ask anyone! I had to do it or she would have exposed me. She would have told the police what I did, and I would spend the rest of my life in jail. I didn't want that—you can understand that, can't you?"

"Who would expose you? For what?"

"Don't act innocent. I know you know what I'm talking about! You went to her hotel room. You told her that I told you all about it. Why would you do something like that? We never had any such conversation. She was furious. There was nothing I could say to calm her down."

Fiona took in a breath. "*Cynthia*! Cynthia made you kill her? Oh my God, Nathan's suspicions were right! I was hoping that he was wrong, but every one of his suspicions were right on the money!"

Tears ran down Calvin's cheeks. "I told her. I felt that after all these years I owed her that much. I was worried that this would be the last time she would be in Pittsburgh, that I would never see her again. So I told her the truth that I was the one who ran her over years ago. I crippled that beautiful talented woman. I hated myself for it! I hated myself for running away. I was afraid. I was afraid that I'd go to prison. I was a coward. But she wasn't upset. I couldn't believe it. She wasn't one bit upset."

The foyer lights came on.

Calvin blinked back. "Do you always have problems with your electrical system?"

"No, not usually."

"Well, I'll tell ya, that basement door was pretty flimsy. I didn't have any problem getting in. The dresser was a hindrance, but not much of one. You really should've had that looked at."

She let out a frustrated sigh. "So I've been told."

Fiona wanted to pull away, except he seemed to be relaxing—even with Harriet pulling and tugging with all of her tiny might, while growling like a Pit Bull. She was kind of proud of the mini but mighty Maltese.

Calvin was letting go, as if he was confessing to a priest—he was releasing himself of his guilt, of his anguish, and more. She had to talk to him in a comforting tone, as if trying to soothe one of her kindergarten students after a fall on the playground.

Quietly, calmly, she asked, "Why…why wasn't she upset, Calvin?"

"She wanted to get even—not so much with me, but with everyone who could do what she couldn't anymore—dance freely, to dance the roles she was born to dance. But that wasn't all of it…" His gaze dropped to the floor as his voice fell away.

"What then? What did she want?" Fiona urged.

"David…not only were the ballerinas beautiful and graceful and whole, but her husband wanted to be near them. He took care of her, but he charmed them, and that made her feel even less. She couldn't stand it anymore."

"So she asked you to kill Alexis?"

His head snapped up. "No! I told you! I didn't kill Miss Alexis! I don't know who killed her—maybe it was Cynthia. I don't know if she killed that lovely girl, but it wouldn't surprise me. All this time she seemed so sweet, so innocent. And then, I made a terrible mistake."

Fiona felt bad for him—he'd been used in the worst manner possible. No matter, he was a murderer, and he was a threat. She knew that she had to keep him calm and keep him talking until someone came. Where were Silja and Officer Dalton? Or maybe Nathan would come soon, but when?

She whispered, "You told her the truth…you told her that you were the one who hit her with your car all those years ago, and you expressed your deep regret."

"Yes…"

"And that's when she insisted that you kill Monroe for her?"

"Not at first. At first she was all understanding and forgiving. It was in the past, she told me. What was done, was done, she said. I gotta tell ya, I felt so blessed, so relieved. And then, she turned on a dime. The day you saw us in the garage—that's when she told me that she wanted to kill Monroe, and that I had to do it for her. She said that Monroe was a self-absorbed shallow woman who was just one of many who'd had a thing with David. Which was true, but Cynthia hated her more than any of the others. I think it was because Cynthia believed that she was going to become PBTs new prima. But the thing is, Monroe wasn't going to be named a principal dancer."

Fiona's eyes widened. "How do you know that?"

"I overheard the Ballet Mistress telling the Ballet Master that she couldn't work with Monroe on that level. She said that Monroe's ego would be unsurmountable. After Miss Silja left, they were going to name a new principal right out of the company. Monroe would've flipped her lid." He blinked and blinked again as if he'd just come out of a trance. "It doesn't matter! I don't want to spend the rest of my life in jail, Fiona! You know too much. Why did you go to Cynthia's room? If you'd stayed away. If you'd stayed quiet, I wouldn't have to do this! Cynthia would've let you live—she likes you, but you are a loose end. I'm sorry."

Fiona tried to jerk her arm away, but he tightened his grip until she thought her arm would break.

"They'll find out, Calvin! Detective Landry already knows! You'll spend your life in jail or maybe worse!"

"Not if I can keep you quiet!" He raised something over his head. In the struggle Fiona couldn't make out what it was, and she wasn't interested in hanging around long enough to find out. She used the only self-defense move that she knew—quickly she curled the fingers on her left hand ramming her knuckles into his right eye. Yelping, Calvin pulled away, grabbing his face, dropping the weapon to the floor with a loud heavy *clang*. Fiona tried to open the door, but he fell against it. She side-stepped him to try to run down the hall to the kitchen door, but even in his tortured state, he had the presence of mind to block her way.

The lights went dark again.

Fiona wasn't sure if that was a good thing or not. Regardless, her options were cut off, except for the stairs. She started up the stairs. Calvin lunged forward in an attempt to tackle her when suddenly the rug was pulled out from under him. Calvin crashed to the floor smashing his face on the hardwood.

Fiona's heart beat like a hammer inside her chest as she ran up the stairs not exactly knowing what she'd do once she reached the top. Jump out a window? Not hardly. Glancing over her shoulder, Harriet was on her heels. Calvin struggled to his feet and was now within three steps away. He lunged forward to grab her, Harriet tucked tail to leap onto the second floor, while

Fiona jumped upward, skipping two steps to land on her hands and knees next to the snarling Maltese. Gathering Harriet up, she rounded the banister to look down to see Calvin clambering up the stairs, and that's when it happened—the staircase began to move! It was moving like an escalator—a downward moving escalator that was dragging Calvin down the stairs toward the foyer! His arms flailed in the air as his feet went off balance with the sudden rapid movement in the opposite direction.

The lights came back on.

Cupping her hand over her mouth, Fiona watched in absolute shock as he thrashed against the descending force that knocked him to his knees. He pushed up only to lose the battle once again, finally falling backward only to have the stairs change direction again. Confused by what just happened, he grabbed the railing. Hand over hand he continued his fight toward the second floor, yet the moment he came within three steps to the top, the escalator rolled backward again, quashing his momentum and his balance.

Looking upward, Fiona said, "Okay, Evelyn, now you're just playing with him."

As if in complete agreement, the stairs began to roll more rapidly. Calvin focused on his feet like a novice log-rolling contestant, and then he let out a loud yelp, pulling his hands away from the railing as if it were on fire, only to tumble head over heels down the staircase. *Thump, thump, thud-a-thump!*

The front door burst open! Detective Landry stepped through with his gun drawn, flanked by Officer Dalton who was followed by several police officers, including Wyatt. They stopped in their tracks when Calvin rolled toward them, landing spread eagle on the hardwood floor at their feet—*bump, bump.*

Groaning and dazed, Calvin grabbed his head.

Wide eyed and slack jawed, Detective Landry took another look at the stairs, but they'd stopped moving. He looked again, not sure he'd actually seen what he thought he saw, and then he yelled, "On your stomach, Kleppner!" Slowly, Calvin complied. The detective looked up the staircase. "Fiona! Fiona, where are you?"

Fiona stepped from behind the banister to stand at the top of the staircase. "I'm right here."

With the officers taking control of Calvin, the detective stepped onto the stairs, hesitating to make sure it was solid, and then rushed to the top, taking Fiona's hands into his. "Are you okay?"

"I'm fine. A little shook up, but I'm fine."

Instantly, Harriet's tail began to wag. Nathan scrubbed his fingers across her head, and then he looked down the stairs, and back at her. "The stairs—they were moving...how did you—"

"You're not going to like the answer. Mmmm, what I mean to say is, you're not going to *believe* me."

Not letting go of her hands, he cocked his head. "Try me."

"Seriously, I'd rather not."

Stepping away, he began to examine the banister. "Where's the switch? I can't believe it, who has an escalator in their house—especially an older home like this?"

"It's unbelievable all right. This house doesn't have an escalator either."

"Then how? I mean, I saw it moving, Fiona. I saw the man flip down the moving staircase."

Wyatt climbed the stairs to join them. "I told you that basement door was going to be problem someday. Sure enough that's how Kleppner got in."

"Did he kick it in?" Nathan asked.

"No, he was more eloquent than that. He used his maintenance man skills, with these…" he held up a screwdriver and a crow bar in his gloved hands. "He simply wedged the crow bar in the jamb and gave a push, the door came right open. No problem, he walked in—even with the dresser in front of it."

Fiona held her hands up in surrender. "Okay, okay, I get it. I need to replace the door. It's first on my list this weekend."

"I don't think so…" Silja called up the stairs, while picking her way past police officers who were examining them trying to figure out why they were moving earlier and not now. When Silja reached the second floor, she asked, "Are you okay? What's going on with the stairs?"

"I'm fine." Fiona whispered in her ear, "Evelyn was taking care of business. I'll explain later."

"Oooh…" Silja said, pitching her a knowing smirk. Nathan regarded them in a suspicious manner. She quickly changed the subject. "Anyway, when I got the all clear to come in and they told me that the case is solved. I called PBT to tell them, and I'm pretty sure that I've convinced them to re-open the show for the weekend. Which means you'll be busy tomorrow at dress rehearsal and you'll be busy on stage Friday, Saturday, and Sunday playing the role of Coppelia. I'm so happy, and I'm sure the ticket holders will be too."

"I'm not so sure," Fiona began. "Calvin admitted that he killed Monroe, but he was adamant that he had nothing to do with Alexis's murder. Nathan, I think I believe him."

"Look, Fiona, I understand. Calvin is an unlikely murder suspect because he's so well known as a nice guy who tries to help everyone out. I'm sure he was blackmailed into the crime, but murderers or desperate people want to get away with what they can. It's bad enough to be charged with one murder, trust me, no one wants to be charged with two. They had motive and they had opportunity. Cynthia has claimed the same thing, but I believe the DA will charge them with both murders."

She turned to Silja, who simply shrugged. Fiona said, "I hear what you're saying, Nathan, but I think he'd be wrong. In any case, now that the murders have been solved, in the DA's eyes, there's really no reason for me to continue in the role of Coppelia—"

"What? You can't back out now, Fiona Quinn! I won't stand for it! And I bet the other dancers won't either. You've got to play the role. You're too cute not to. Isn't that right, Detective Dream—er—um, Landry?" Silja said.

"She's right. You've done all the rehearsing. Why wouldn't you want to see it through?" Nathan asked.

Fiona looked at Nathan, to Silja, and then back at Nathan. Letting out a sigh of surrender, she said, "I suppose you're right. Besides I don't see how I can say no. It seems I'm outnumbered."

Silja looped her arm through Nathan's. "You got that right, sister."

Looking down the stairs, they realized that the police had cleared out, taking Calvin with them. Red and blue flashing lights sped down Oxford Street. One officer poked his head through the front door. "Couldn't find anything down here to make the steps move."

"There's nothing up here either." Nathan glanced at Fiona. "Guess it was our *imagination*."

"Yeah…guess it was Kleppner's too," The officer muttered as he slipped outside.

"I'll take it from here, Landry," Wyatt said.

"Make sure the coroner gets that crow bar. I gotta feelin' he's used it before—like on Monroe McCarthy."

"Will do." Wyatt nodded at the girls, and then trotted down the stairs and out the front door.

Nathan turned to Fiona. "How about that coffee?"

"It's all ready. Have a seat in the living room, I'll bring it in," Fiona said with a demure smile on her lips.

Silja made a big show of yawning and stretching her back. "Oh, I'm bushed. Too much excitement for one day for me, I'm afraid. Think I'll go to bed." Turning, she shot a quick wink at her friend.

"Have you heard from Grant?" Fiona asked.

"No, but Clark said he's hopeful that I will very soon."

"So you made the forbidden phone call?"

"Grant will just have to find a way to forgive me." With that, she kissed Fiona on the cheek and then went to her bedroom.

—⚬⚬⚬—

Fiona carried a tray filled with coffee, creamer, sugar, a plate of cookies, and an envelope into the living room where Nathan was sitting on the couch with Harriet on his lap. "Harriet seems to really like you."

"That's good. My mom always says that if a dog doesn't like someone, that's someone you should be wary of."

"I totally agree with your mom. Dogs are very good judges of character." She sat the tray on the coffee table and kissed the little dog on the head. "She's my hero. She really stood her ground when Calvin was threatening me. I'm so proud of her." She poured Nathan a mug of coffee.

"I take it black," Nathan supplied. She handed him the mug and the envelope from the tray. "What's this?"

Fiona had no doubt that she was turning a brilliant shade of red. "A ticket for Friday's performance of Coppelia. When the show was cancelled because of the murders, I was keeping it for posterity, but now that the show is back on…um…I was hoping that you'd like to come see the show."

Saying nothing, Nathan stared at the envelope for a moment, and then his lips curled. "Thank you, I'm honored."

"Have you ever been to the ballet?"

"No, but there's always a first time for everything, and I'll actually know a ballerina in the show."

"Oh…I'm not a ballerina. Well, I could've been, if I hadn't had that accident. Whatever made me go skiing anyway? I didn't know how to ski. How stupid was that?" Taking in a breath, she sighed. "To think I could've been wearing tutus and tiaras and taking curtain calls and traveling. But hey, I like being a kindergarten teacher—really I do. I guess things happen for a reason. I guess I was meant to be a—"

Nathan took her hands into his. "Fiona…you'll always be a ballerina to me."

She could feel the heat in her cheeks. Why was she always turning red in the presence of this man? She favored him with a bashful smile.

Clearing his throat, Nathan said, "Now…about that staircase—"

Yikes.

Twelve

"Tendu, two, three, four, five, six, seven, and eight, degage, degage, degage..." the Ballet Master called out to the gathering of dancers spread across the stage taking a quick class to warm up and focus their minds on the task before them—the last rehearsal for the final weekend performances of Coppelia. His hair had been powdered white and a close beard had been attached to his jaw for the role of Dr. Coppelius. Fiona felt badly that David Sheppard would not be playing the role after she had worked with him at length to prepare for this night and the three pending performances. She also felt that he was responsible for the ease she was feeling at this moment amongst the dancers, warming up as one of them, and the confidence she was experiencing that all would work out with her new partner.

In fact, a sense of sadness swirled among the dancers because David would not be part of the show. Many speculated that he would no longer perform, that he would be too ashamed of what his wife had done, and unable to face the ballet community ever again. How sad.

Throughout the rehearsal exhaustion was taking its toll. Fiona was desperate for a good night's sleep. She hadn't slept a wink last night thinking about Calvin's desperate confession and even more desperate renunciation that he had anything to do with Alexis's death. He was so passionate in his denial. His eyes looked so truthful. If he were lying, wouldn't she be able to recognize that? Fiona believed that she would.

Perhaps Cynthia killed Alexis, but Nathan said that she was denying it as well. So who? Evan? Did Evan kill his sister, and if so, what could have gone on that he would kill his own blood? Over the years, she had been very angry with her brother, but she never felt the need to kill him—although she had threatened a time or two.

No, she didn't believe that Calvin had killed Alexis.

"Very nice," the Ballet Master said, breaking through her thoughts. "You will have twenty minutes more for stretching, twenty more to get dressed, and then rehearsal will begin."

Fiona felt a gentle hand cup her shoulder.

"Are you nervous?" Silja asked.

"Surprisingly, no," she replied.

"Good. Just relax and have a good time. I'm so glad we're dancing together again. It's like old times."

Fiona enjoyed the lively chatter in the dressing room under the bright lights stationed above the long line of mirrors over the vanities. The ballerinas talked and laughed while unerringly applying their makeup and tiaras. Silja and several of the dancers helped Fiona draw up her hair in a severe bun and put on her makeup, including the wings at the end of the thick line of eyeliner and the sparkly false eyelashes. When they were finished, she barely recognized the reflection staring back at her from the mirror. She looked like…a ballerina!

Soon costumes were plucked from the racks, pointe shoes were tied around the dancer's ankles, and then they hurried to the backstage for rehearsal. It was all so exhilarating. Fiona couldn't believe that she was back amongst the pre-show excitement. It felt good. She'd forgotten how good. She'd forgotten how much she missed it all. Silja was right. It was like old times.

"Attention!" Ballet Mistress Adele called over the din. "Attention girls!" The room went quiet. "We've had a few very rough days and week. Our lovely ballet company has lost two wonderful dancers. My heart is heavy, as I'm sure yours is as well. But Coppelia has been saved, and we will dance this beautiful ballet in their honor." The ballerinas clapped. She hushed them again. "That said, I felt now was a good time to announce that our very own Sara Holloway will take on the position that Alexis left vacant—principal dancer number one. I will announce a soloist in a day or so." Many of the dancers enveloped Sara in their arms whispering congratulations. Sara beamed with pride.

"How nice for Sara," Silja whispered to Fiona. "She's such a hard worker. She always arrives before everyone else."

With narrowed eyes, Fiona cocked her head to one side. "Yeah…I remember you telling me that before."

The backstage was buzzing with congratulatory hugs and kisses, and then suddenly a hush weaved throughout the group. The dancers craned their necks to see what was happening on stage. Fiona tried to see over their heads, but couldn't, and then a soft round of applause began to grow, and grow, and grow.

What was going on? Why were the dancers clapping their hands? Why were their faces brightening into wide smiles?

"Look, Fiona," one of the dancers dressed as a peasant girl said. "Your partner is back!"

"What?"

Fiona finally saw David Sheppard making his way through the group toward her, until he was standing in front of her wearing a wary expression.

"David…are you going to dance with us?" She was breathless with joy. "Seriously? You're going to be in the show?"

He looked at the floor and then slowly dragged his gaze to meet hers. "If you'll have me. I can't apologize enough for what has been brought upon this company, and I can't express how deeply sorry I am for what happened to Alexis and Monroe. I cannot excuse myself from all blame. I will carry that part of it with me forever, but please know that I had no physical hand in their deaths, and if you'll forgive me, I'd like to dance the role of Dr. Coppelius—even if it's just one last time."

"Cynthia—how is she doing?" Fiona asked.

"I don't know. She won't see me," he said, gloom filling his tone. "She and Calvin are in the Allegheny County jail waiting to be arraigned—most likely on Monday."

"I'm so sorry, David." Fiona looked around at the faces of the dancers. Were they leaving this decision in her hands? Why? It didn't really matter. Taking in their beseeching eyes, she knew what they wanted her to say, and if she were to be totally honest, it was exactly how she was feeling too.

"We'd love you to dance with us, David, and I hope it's not the last time for you." David wrapped his arms around her, squeezing her tightly. Over his shoulder, Fiona saw Sara slip away from the backstage area into the hallway that led to the dressing rooms. She released the embrace. "Excuse me, I have to do something. I'll be back in just a moment."

The dancers surrounded David as she made her way toward the same exit that Sara had taken. She looked up and down the hallway. Sara was nowhere in sight, but Fiona had a gut feeling that she knew where the young dancer had gone. Quickly, she untied her pointe shoes, laid them just outside the stage entrance, and then padded down the hallway to what once was Alexis Cartwright's dressing room. She was always in tune with the phantoms who walked these halls, but today there seemed to be a different entity present, following her with purpose. As she drew closer to the room, she could feel the sensation of someone just behind her, and she could feel that they desperately wanted her to continue forward.

The door to the dressing room was closed. The crime tape had been broken and was limply dangling to the floor. She didn't hear it—she felt a soft sigh, only it wasn't her own, at this point she believed it belonged to Alexis. Biting her lip, she laid her ear to the door. She could hear someone talking, but she couldn't make out their words. Ever so cautiously, she took hold of the doorknob, twisted it and opened the door just a tiny gap.

She peeked into the room. Only a small table lamp had been lit, favoring the room with a soft glow. Sara stood at the vanity admiring the dimmed lights above. She ran her hands over the mirror, and then her eyes fell upon the empty vase just left of the mirror. She took a moment to readjust the position of the vase closer to the mirror. From Fiona's perspective, the new spot for the vase seemed to suit Sara better—for whatever reason. Then she gently smoothed her fingers over the garment rack. A smile stretching across her face,

Sara pressed up onto her pointe shoes to bouree in a tiny circle of celebration.

"You've done it, Sara Holloway," she whispered out loud, performing a swift entrechat. "All your hard work paid off. All the hours of barre work and stretching—it all worked out. Everything you've ever wanted is about to come true." She pulled out the vanity chair and sat down, caressing the vanity top with the palms of her hands. She closed her eyes. Serenity filling her expression. "It's all mine now. And they don't even suspect. No, no one suspects innocent, quiet, hard-working, Sara Holloway. She wouldn't hurt anyone for her own gain. She wouldn't hurt a flea." She rose from the chair to run her hands across the costumes still hanging on the rack. "But if I hadn't killed Alexis, I'd still be waiting. Who knows how long I'd wait for the opportunity to be the principal? I'd waited long enough." She looked to the ceiling as if Alexis were up there somewhere within ear shot. "I'm sorry, Alexis, but you should've taken the offer from the Chicago Ballet last month. If you had, you'd still be alive right now. I wouldn't have had to…kill you. I feel bad, really I do, but you had your chance, and I took mine."

"So you're just going to let Calvin and Cynthia take the blame for a murder that they didn't commit?" Fiona said, as she stepped inside the room.

Slack jawed, Sara whirled around. "What are you doing here? How long have you been standing there?"

"Long enough. You can't do this, Sara."

She chuckled. "You don't recognize me. Do you, Fiona?"

Again, Fiona studied her face. She was certain that she'd met Sara before when they'd bumped into her in the hallway before finding Alexis's body, but she couldn't place her—and she still couldn't.

"I'm Amber Archer. I used to dance with you and Silja here at PBT years ago."

Gasping, Fiona's eyes flooded with recognition. "Amber...yes, I recognize you now. You used to be a blonde."

"And twenty-five pounds heavier. I didn't want to return to Pittsburgh with people remembering how much the dance mistresses hated me. Not to mention the incident with the magnesia and Mistress Gisela. They tossed me out of PBT. My parents were so embarrassed. We moved to Philadelphia. They wanted me to give up dancing. They wanted me to become a teacher of all things. Can you believe that?"

Fiona's spine stiffened. She blinked back. "There are worse things to be than a *teacher*—"

"Not as far as I'm concerned. I lost the weight. I worked hard and continued to dance. But I wanted to start a new life, with a fresh reputation and a fresh name. I had to come back here because the opportunities were so amazing. I knew I could snag a principal role. I knew I could prove to the dancers of Pittsburgh that I was good."

"Look, it doesn't matter if your name is Amber or Sara, you can't let someone else take the blame for a murder that *you* committed."

"Why not?"

"Be—because it's wrong!"

Sara flipped her arms out. "Murder in general is *wrong*, Fiona. But I made the commitment. Look, *they* killed Monroe—Calvin and Cynthia. I can't begin to tell you how convenient that was. It was all too easy. After I killed Alexis with Cynthia's cane, I planted it in a place where it would be easily found. Of course, after I'd wiped it clean with alcohol. But I didn't stop there. I even threw the bottle of alcohol away in Calvin's trash bin, hoping someone would find it. At the funeral, I bought myself a little insurance policy. I swayed a boatload of suspicion toward Alexis's brother by saying that I saw him leave her dressing room after hearing them argue. And yes, he did visit her that day, and yes, I did see him leave, but they didn't argue. Not a bit—but it made him an instant suspect."

"I'll bet you hit Silja over the head too."

"I did. But that was just for fun. I have to admit that I considered killing her, but someone came along."

"Well the fun's over now, Sara…er…Amber, or whatever your name is! You can't do this! I won't let you do this! I'm going to set the record straight. You won't be dancing a principal role anytime soon. You'll be sitting in a jail cell just like Calvin and Cynthia are." Fiona spun on her heels toward the door.

"I don't think so!" Sara said, grabbing the vase from the vanity to smack Fiona over the head.

Shattered glass rained over the floor. Fiona fell against the door as the room spun. She clung to the door knob, trying to pull herself up and to hold on to consciousness, but the room was getting darker and darker and darker, until Sara pushed her to the floor.

—ɷ—

Locking the door, Sara stood over Fiona trying to come up with a workable plan. Fiona knew the truth. She had to keep her quiet. No—she had to get rid of her, except she also had to be in rehearsal within the next few minutes, and she couldn't be late or people would come looking for her—and Fiona.

She rushed to the vanity to open the drawer. Sara smiled. She'd hit pay-dirt. Among a brush, hairpins, a case of eyelashes, and an unopened card of hairbands, there lay several fresh bundles of pointe shoe ribbon. Sara grabbed the bundles. Upon removing the thin metal clip, she rolled the ribbon out. It was long and new and strong. Stretching it out and giving it a good snap between her fists, she made her way toward Fiona, laying on the floor, unconscious and helpless.

Thirteen

As covertly as possible, Sara eased the door open to peek into the hallway. Finding it empty, she stepped out of the dressing room, closed the door, and then carefully replaced the yellow crime scene tape over the threshold. Smoothing her Juliet-length skirt and a few errant strands of hair that had come loose from her bun, she quickened down the corridor toward the backstage door, hoping that she hadn't been missed. As she yanked the door open, she almost smashed right into Silja.

"Oops!" Silja exclaimed. "I'm sorry, we're just about to get the rehearsal started. Have you seen Fiona?"

She hadn't quite prepared for questions so soon, but she had to come up with something quickly, or she'd be found out. "Fiona…oh, yes, I just saw her a few minutes ago. Um…er…I hate to be the one to have to tell you this, but…um…she left."

"What? She left? Why would she leave? We need to rehearse the show—"

"Well that's just it. I saw her heading for the door, and when I asked her where she was going, she said that she simply didn't want to play the role of Coppelia. She said it was too…nerve-wracking, and she felt badly, but she couldn't go through with it. Poor thing, she was shaking like a leaf."

"I don't believe it!" Silja tried to sidestep Sara. "I have to stop her—"

"No! I mean...I tried to stop her, really I did, but she was insistent. I think if she feels that strongly about it. We should let her go. Really I do."

Silja cupped her hand over her mouth in disbelief and disappointment. "What will we tell Mistress Adele?"

Sara put her arm around Silja, feigning compassion for her fellow dancer. "C'mon...I'll go with you. Don't worry, it'll be hard, but she'll find a replacement for her—she'll have to. Everything will work out okay, you'll see." She led a distraught Silja into the backstage area, feeling that she'd dodged a bullet—for now. How many more bullets would there be, and how would she hold it all at bay?

—⁓—

Fiona's eyelids felt as though they weighed fifty pounds apiece as she tried to open them. Her head was thumping, and her hands were numb. She tried to move her hands only to find them bound together. When she tried to move her feet, she made the same discovery. The tiny space where she'd been stuffed was dark. She could feel boxes piled up around her, and clothing pressing against her shoulders and head. Although she was fighting for consciousness, she realized that she must be in a closet—probably in Alexis's dressing room.

The sound of the orchestra playing was muted by the closed doors. A shudder of alarm rushed through her—the rehearsal had begun! In a panic, she shimmied around in an attempt to stand, but the banging in her head put a stop to any quick movements.

How could they be conducting the rehearsal without her? Surely they noticed that she was not present—especially Silja. Why would they not come looking for her? Then again, she was in the closet of a dead woman's dressing room. Why would anyone look there? One thing was for certain—Sara wouldn't disclose her location any time soon. For that matter, what did Sara plan to do with her after the rehearsal was over?

Fiona gasped. Sara was really left with only one option—she would have to kill her of course. Sara had confessed to killing Alexis Cartwright. She would have no choice but to get rid of her as well.

Goodness, last week she was an ordinary every day kindergarten teacher. Now it seemed that everyone wanted her dead—Calvin, Cynthia, and now Sara or Amber Archer, as it were. Evelyn had helped her escape Calvin's attempt on her life, but in this instance, she was on her own.

Taking in a braced breath, Fiona moved around until she was on her knees. She was forced to rest for a moment or two in order to let the thumping in her brain to subside—at least a little. Finally, she found the strength to lean against the back of the closet and shimmy her back up the wall until she was standing. It was tight, but she made it happen. Again she rested, pressing her head against the door. If she didn't get out she could very well end up floating down the Ohio River.

Using her shoulder, she pushed against the door. It didn't budge. She pushed again—nothing. As she continued to push and shove, she realized that something was wedged against the door. Perhaps Sara had put a chair under the door knob. It was solid.

"Hey!" She yelled. "Hey! Is anybody out there?" She listened—no one answered. Of course not, everyone went to rehearsal. She had no idea how long she'd been in the closet. Perhaps they did come looking—or perhaps Sara told them some story to cover her tracks. Sara had proven that she was a pretty convincing liar.

Trying not to panic, Fiona laid her head against the door. Someone had to find her—they just had to—or it would be curtains for her!

—⟶⟜⟵—

The orchestra played the final notes of the first half of the show as the curtain lowered. "All right everyone.

Very well done! Let's take a fifteen minute break, and then we'll continue with the second half of the show," Mistress Adele said.

Everyone relaxed out of their closing poses to head for the backstage area where bottles of water were waiting on a table. Silja turned to David. "I can't imagine why Fiona would abandon the show at the last moment. It's not like her, David. It's not like her at all."

"I didn't think so either, Silja, but you heard what Sara said, the girl just couldn't handle her nerves. Maybe we put too much pressure on her. Perhaps we should have released her from this responsibility when the police investigation ended, and they rescheduled the show."

"No, I don't believe it. Something's not right," Silja grabbed a bottle of water from the table and then walked into the hallway. Taking a good swig of water, she looked up and then down. Only a few dancers were milling about. Letting out a frustrated breath, she hurried to the dressing room. Her cell phone was lying on her vanity. She sent a quick text:

Fiona, please come back. Let's talk about this.

She carried the cell toward the door with her in hopes that Fiona would reply quickly. As she was about to step into the hallway, there was a loud *tweet, tweet*. She stopped. A text message had just been received—somewhere in the room. She whirled around to look at the coat rack—and there it was, Fiona's coat was still hanging on the rack. Silja's eyes narrowed. Fiona would never go out into the weather without a coat—she was too… too… teacherish for that kind of nonsense.

Silja marched over to the coat and snatched it from the hanger. Sure enough, Fiona's knit cap with a pair of gloves stuffed inside was cradled in the sleeve. Yep, even when Fiona wasn't with her students, she practiced what she preached—keep your stuff together in an organized fashion, and this time it had paid off—in a big way. Quickly, she dialed Fiona's cell number. A nanosecond later there was a ringing sounding through the room. Indeed, Fiona's cell phone was somewhere in the room! Silja set to following the sound until she found her missing friend's backpack stuffed under her assigned vanity space. Fiona hadn't left. Silja knew it couldn't be so. Fiona Quinn was true blue to the core. She would never let her friends down. She opened the backpack to rifle through it until she came up with the device that now fell silent, moving on to voice mail mode.

Staring at her friend's cell phone, trepidation crowded Silja's chest. Maybe Fiona was right. Maybe someone else had killed Alexis, and maybe that person was lurking in the theater right now. Flipping Fiona's coat back on the rack, she hurried into the hallway. Fiona had to be somewhere in the theater, but where? There were so many little corridors and rooms and places that the dancers or orchestra members or the audience never saw or knew about.

Silja came to a complete and sudden halt.

Wait just a minute.

Why would Sara tell her that Fiona had left?

Why would she make up such a story?

That's when the epiphany punched her square in the nose—they had an understudy for Monroe, they easily placed a seasoned dancer in Fiona's spot, but Sara was now joyfully dancing Alexis's role, and she would be dancing all her roles from now on!

Silja was almost at a dead run as she approached the stage door. She slid to a stop when she saw a pair of pointe shoes lying in the hallway—just outside the backstage door. Several of the dancers were rushing back to the rehearsal.

"Whose shoes are these?" she asked the girls who were all wearing theirs.

"Don't know," one dancer said. "They've been lying there since the rehearsal began. I had to go back to the dressing room for something, and they were sitting there at that time." The girls didn't wait for her reaction and slipped through the stage door.

Pressing several buttons on Fiona's cell, Silja's thumbs raced through her contacts. Finding the number she needed, she tapped the contact. "C'mon Detective Dreamboat, answer your phone."

Fourteen

Evan Cartwright let out a frustrated sigh when he opened his apartment door to find Detective Landry on the other side. Crossing his arms over his chest, he fell against the jamb. "What can I do for you, Detective?"

"I've been trying to imagine how I would feel if my parents left all their possessions and money to my sister. I mean, nobody's perfect, right? You made a few mistakes. Okay, maybe some *big* mistakes, but you'd think that parents would find a way to forgive. Maybe not forget, but *forgive*. My mom is very forgiving, but that doesn't mean she's forgotten about the bay window that I broke with a baseball when I was twelve. She reminds me about it every time we watch a Pirate's game."

"Pfft, it's obvious that you never met my parents, Detective. Alexis was the golden girl. I was the total screw-up. And no, they were not forgiving or forgetful."

"Well, in their defense, your rap sheet is a half-mile long—DUI's, drug charges, robbery, stealing a car—"

"But the one thing you didn't see on that sheet was murder, and that's because I've never murdered anyone, including my sister. Besides, I saw on the news that they've made two arrests for Alexis's murder and that other dancer too. So unless you're here to apologize for jumping to conclusions, I'm kinda busy—"

Evan attempted to step back into his apartment and close the door, but Nathan caught it with his ha. "I'm not in the habit of apologizing, Mr. Cartwright. That said, something doesn't feel right about those two suspects that we've got in custody. So I've decided to re-check my facts along with my suspects."

"I've told you everything there is to tell. I went to see my sister before the show. She was alive. We visited for a short time because I was late for an appointment. I returned to see if she'd like to go to lunch. She said no. I felt badly, but she was still alive when I left. Someone killed her. It wasn't me."

"Did you see anyone else at the theater? I mean, during the second visit—on your way in, or on your way out?"

"No…wait…yes! There was a woman. She was coming down the hall when I was leaving Alexis's dressing room."

"Was she a dancer or a janitress?"

"Oh, she was *definitely* a dancer. She was wearing a black leotard and tights and pointe shoes—the whole package."

"Did she go in to see your sister?"

Raking his fingers through his hair, Evan searched his mind. "I'm not sure. But now that I think about it, she was heading in that general direction, but I was in a hurry—"

Just then the detective's cell phone rang. He looked down to see the screen announce—Fiona Quinn. "Hello…"

"Nathan, thank God I caught you," Silja began. "You need to come to the Benedum right away. Fiona's missing. I think something terrible has happened to her, and I'm fairly sure that I know who's responsible."

"Slow down, Silja. What's going on?"

"They announced Alexis's replacement today—Sara Holloway. Remember her? She's the girl who said that she heard Alexis and her brother arguing. Anyway, shortly after the announcement, Fiona was gone. Sara told us that she'd changed her mind about dancing in the show and left. I didn't believe it. And now I know she didn't leave—her coat, backpack, and cell phone were still in the dressing room when we took a break, and I found what I believe are her pointe shoes in the hall." Silja hesitated, taking in a breath. "I think Fiona was right. Someone else had it in for Alexis, and it wasn't her brother. I think it was Sara Holloway. You've got to come right away."

"I'm on my way, but listen to me, Silja. *Do not* approach Sara. If she is Alexis's murderer, and if she did harm Fiona, she's capable of harming anyone. Stay clear, and wait for me to get there."

"Okay, but hurry, Nathan. There's really not much rehearsal left. I've gotta go." With that Silja hung up.

Immediately, he thumbed a number into his phone. "Wyatt…get Dalton, and get to the Benedum. No lights. No sirens. Just park and wait for me. We've got trouble." Upon Wyatt's confirmation, he turned to Evan. "C'mon, Cartwright, I might need you to identify that dancer."

"Getting into downtown from here is gonna be tricky, Detective. It's Friday night on the South Side. Traffic's gonna be a real bear," Evan pointed out, as he pulled his apartment door closed.

"Don't I know it?"

—⟋⟋⟍—

"Hey!" Fiona called for the hundredth time. Her throat was dry, and her voice was more of a croak than a yell at this point. It was no use anyway. No one could hear her. The old theater's walls were thick and so were the doors. She listened to the distant whirr of the orchestra beginning to play the second half of the show. She had to get out of the closet. When the rehearsal ended Sara would come back, and who knew what plan she'd concocted to get rid of her by now. She had to concentrate on freeing her hands rather than getting someone's attention.

She twisted and pulled and wrangled her wrists. She needed to calm down and feel what Sara had used to tie her wrists together. After all, it's not like rope was a typical item one would find laying around in the dancer's dressing areas. At least she didn't remember ever seeing any.

She ran the binding over her cheek. It was smooth and soft. It only took a moment for her to realize that Sara had bound her up with pointe shoe ribbon. Alexis must've kept extra in her vanity drawers. Now that made sense. Ribbon was something that was quite common to find lying about. Wow. The pink stuff was strong and it was tight, but the good news was that with a little finagling, or maybe a lot of finagling, it would eventually stretch. It would be difficult since it was tied so tautly, and it felt as though Sara had used several layers of ribbon, but she had to make it work. Her life depended on it.

Forcing her hands into fists, she scrubbed her knuckles together while her wrists moved back and forth, outward and inward, and up and down. The ribbon dug into her skin, quickly making her wrists raw and sore. The pain would be a small price to pay in exchange for her safety. At the same time, she tried as best she could to march in place—little tiny steps to pull on the ribbons around her ankles to make them stretch and hopefully give. It wasn't the best plan—she fell down against a pile of boxes that were currently poking her in the ribs, adding to her discomfort—throbbing head, raw wrists, aches and pains in general. Now she would spend who knows how long climbing over the boxes to get back up.

Ugh!

———ɷ———

The rehearsal was going way too smoothly. Many of the dancers had danced in a production of Coppelia at one point or other during their careers. David was so familiar with the role of Dr. Coppelius that he could probably dance it in a coma if necessary.

Sara was dancing so eloquently that it was making Silja sick. She wanted nothing more than to chasse over to her, punch her in the jaw, and then force her to tell her where Fiona was. No—Detective Landry told her to steer clear of Sara, and that's exactly what she planned to do. She just hoped that he arrived soon—there wasn't much of the show left to rehearse.

Standing behind the curtain, stage right, David came up from behind to whisper in her ear. "What's wrong, Silja? You seem so tense. I'm the one with a wife in jail, what's going on?"

"We have to slow down the rehearsal, David."

"Why on earth would you want to do that?"

"Because Sara Holloway killed Alexis Cartwright." David took a step backward.

Silja explained, "Fiona hasn't left the theater. She's here somewhere. Sara has her stashed because Fiona knows the truth. I don't know how Sara knows it, but Fiona's in trouble, and we can't let Sara leave the theater without finding out what has happened to Fiona."

"If you're sure, we really shouldn't be playing around with this, Silja. We need to call the police. I hate to do it, but we should call Detective Landry."

"I already have. He's on his way, but we've got to do something in the meantime."

"I'm in. What do you suggest?"

"I think it's time to add a little slapstick to this classic ballet."

David glanced over his shoulder to see Mistress Adele watching the dancers on stage. He sighed. "Poor Adele. She's had so much stress over this production." He looked across the stage to see Sara waiting for her cue. Smiling he said, "Oh well, one must do what one must do. Go get her."

The music slowed indicating an eerie scene. Tossing David a quick wink, Silja stepped onto the stage, pretending to sneak toward Dr. Coppelius's shop, while Sara entered from stage left. Silja made a change to the choreography. As she approached the shop, she stepped into a combination of quick turns—pique, pique, chaine, chaine, pique—plowing right into Sara, knocking her to the floor. *Thud!* Using her acting skills, Silja contrived a startled reaction and set to pulling Sara from the floor, as if to gracefully save the scene.

Sara glanced at Mistress Adele who was standing very rigid with her hands planted on her hips. Cleary, the woman was not happy, but evidently she was willing to allow for the mistake as she made no attempt to stop the rehearsal. Sara let Silja pull her upright and continued to act as if they were breaking into the doll maker's shop.

Carefully, Silja made a big show of prying at the door as the music grew more suspenseful, and then she yanked it open, smacking Sara in the face. "Ouch!" Sara squealed, stumbling backward a step or two before regaining her balance. She looked offstage. Mistress Adele had missed that move, she was busy helping one of the dancers with a costume snafu. The dancers waiting behind the curtains and those positioned in the shop as dolls hadn't missed anything. They were watching slack-jawed at Silja's mishaps.

Silja continued into the shop, tiptoeing about, pretending to look for the beautiful maiden, Coppelia. Out of the corner of her eye, she could see Sara cautiously following her.

There's more where that came from, honey, Silja mused.

Returning to the proper choreography, Silja allowed Sara to become comfortable while they searched

Dr. Coppelius's shop, luring her into a false faith that the accidents were nothing more than just that.

The orchestra cued that something even more gripping was about to happen. Dr. Coppelius was making his entrance, pulling his key from the pocket of his vest, showing it to the absent audience, and then searching for the keyhole in the door. The door jiggled—he was coming in! Silja spun on her heels to shove Sara into the dancers posing as dolls along the wall of the shop. Shocked by the move, the dancers caught Sara only to toss her back toward Silja, who pitched her sideways and then rushed to find a hiding place in an ornate armoire next to the door. She flung open the doors of the armoire to reveal where Coppelia was sitting.

As she stepped inside the armoire, Silja saw Mistress Adele grab her head, flabbergasted by the peculiar antics. As she pulled the doors of the armoire closed, she could see Sara's face turning redder and redder with each faux calamity. Like the orchestra, Sara's temper was rising to a crescendo, and David hadn't put his two cents in—yet.

—◦◦◦—

"We're in position. Where are you, Landry?" Wyatt asked the moment the detective answered his cell.

"Traffic is a nightmare. I'm using my lights, and I have had to use the sirens every so often, but it's still slow-going," he explained as he drove up behind a red sports car. Letting out an irritated sigh, he turned on the siren. The young couple in the car jumped, then pulled the car to the side giving Nathan passage.

"What do you want us to do?"

"I'm hoping to be there within five minutes or so. Hold tight." He turned on his sirens once again in hopes of closing the distance between him and the Benedum.

—⁂—

After pushing and pulling at boxes, and telling herself that there were no spiders or creepy crawlies of any kind among them, Fiona finally made it up on her feet once again. The ribbons around her wrists were indeed starting to stretch and give but not without causing painful friction burns. While she couldn't see the bruises, she could feel the burn. The small space was starting to feel stuffy as if she'd sucked all the oxygen out. Even though she didn't normally have problems with closed in spaces, she was starting to feel quite claustrophobic.

Running her knuckles along the length of the door, she hooked the ribbons over the door knob and began pulling. The old sturdy door shook but did not give. The ribbons dug into her thumb joint. She winced but kept tugging at the knob, hoping that the layers of ribbons would soon be forced over her hand, and then she would begin the next challenge: figuring out how to get out of the closet.

She couldn't be sure what Sara's plans for her were when the rehearsal was over. She was well aware that Sara couldn't afford to let her go—she knew the truth, and yes, she would tell. Would Sara leave the theater with everyone else and then return with help? These thoughts were not helpful at all. Trying to quell her rising fear, she pulled and tugged until she thought the skin on her wrists would peel from the bone. Fiona was certain of two things: no one knew where she was, and time was running out.

The rehearsal seemed to have returned to a normal pace since David had stepped onto the set. Sara was relieved and it appeared that the Ballet Mistress was as well. What was going on with Silja? Was she that upset over Fiona or had she figured out that she had a hand in her disappearance? Sara had to get a plan in place to get rid of Fiona after rehearsal was over and everyone went home. Her stomach was in knots. If she didn't take care of business quickly, Silja would realize for certain that Fiona hadn't gone home. It was hard to think and dance at the same time.

David approached the armoire and in a sweeping dramatic fashion, he opened the doors to expose Silja now dressed as Coppelia, sitting on a small stool with book in hand, and an absent expression on her face. He raised his arms in grand *'abracadabra'* showmanship. Instantly, Silja snapped her eyes open. She jerked to life in a robotic manner.

Sara held her hiding position, waiting for the cue to make her move, except as Silja stepped into her dance with David, she saw Detective Landry talking to Mistress Adele off stage. She glanced at Silja who nodded in her direction for the detective. Panic ripped through her. She'd been had! Somehow Silja had figured it out. She didn't have time to consider the hows of the matter. She had to escape.

Calmly, so as to not disrupt the rehearsal, the detective pointed to her and then wiggled his finger, indicating that he wanted her to make her way to the backstage area. The Ballet Mistress looked overtly distraught. Sara could almost read the poor woman's mind, *Could anything else possibly go wrong with this show?* The answer was a resounding, *yes!*

Sara slowly lifted from her hiding place beneath Dr. Coppelius's workbench to give the impression that she was going to the backstage area, while Silja and David continued their dance. As she drew closer, Silja stepped into promenade position. David held her hand to turn her gracefully in a circle, except Sara grabbed

Silja by the other hand to shove her into David who lost his balance and they both crashed into the open armoire!

The dancers on and off stage gasped. Sara took off at a dead run toward stage left. Her pointe shoes clapping nosily over the floor. Detective Landry rushed across the stage after her, dodging dancers, jumping over Silja and David now clambering out of the armoire. When Sara reached the backstage at left, she grabbed a lever and pulled it down. One of the overhead booms that held the backdrop of the charming little town came crashing down right in front of the detective, trapping him in the heavy canvas, blocking his passage.

Dancers screamed and scattered to get out of the way, while Sara darted through the darkness of the backstage toward stage right. Struggling to unbury himself from the dense fabric of the drop, Detective Landry jumped to his feet to once again wind his way through exasperated dancers to continue the chase.

Sara glanced over her shoulder to see the detective gaining. As she passed the table filled with bottles of water, full and empty, she flipped it over in his path. Plastic bottles bounced and rolled over the stage area. In her frustration, Mistress Adele picked one up and hurled it at Sara, hitting her in the shoulder. The detective tripped over them as he tried to maneuver through, and scrambled to his feet.

Too late now. It was most obvious that they knew of her involvement with Alexis Cartwright's death. Forget Fiona Quinn—it didn't matter anymore if she got rid of her or not—the truth had been exposed. It was all about self-preservation now. She had to get out of the theater, get lost in the city, find a place to think, and then get out of Pittsburgh undetected.

Shoving stunned dancers aside, she grabbed the stage door to push through into the hallway only to feel a body slam into hers knocking her to the floor. Detective Landry dove on top of her. They fell through the stage door into the hallway.

"Is this our girl, Landry?" an officer asked, offering the detective a hand, while pulling a pair of handcuffs from his belt.

"I wouldn't have tackled her if she wasn't, would I, Wyatt?"

"Hope not."

The detective climbed to his feet. He stood over Sara. "Where is Fiona Quinn?"

"I want a lawyer." The ballerina said, while Wyatt slapped the cuffs on her wrists.

From behind, Silja rushed toward Sara. Detective Landry caught her by the waist. Kicking and struggling, Silja cried out, "Give me five minutes with her! I'm not a cop. I don't have to abide by any ethical code or guidelines! I'll get her to tell us what happened to Fiona!"

"Easy, Silja! Easy! We'll find her!" the detective said.

Sara did not cower away from Silja. She didn't as much as blink. She simply stared forward and repeated, "I want a lawyer."

When Silja was calm enough to be set free, she pointed at Sara. "She better be living and breathing, Sara. Or these police officers won't be able to hold me back." With that, Detective Landry gestured for Wyatt to take Sara away—for her own safety, and to protect Silja's good citizenship.

They followed Wyatt and Sara into the hallway. Evan Cartwright nodded. "That's the woman, Detective Landry. That's the woman I saw going toward Alexis's dressing room last week."

"Thanks, Evan. Now we need to find Fiona Quinn."

"I want to help," Evan said. Officer Dalton joined the group.

"We appreciate all the help we can get. Spread out everyone. She has to be somewhere in this theater. Sara didn't have time to take her out, did she?"

"I can't imagine how. The rehearsal started rather quickly. Sara wasn't late," Silja said.

"Let's go," the detective said. Immediately everyone, including David, Mistress Adele, and the dancers set out in all directions to look for Fiona. As the detective turned to make his way down the hallway, his eyes were drawn to Alexis Cartwright's dressing room. Instantly, as if someone had tugged it, the crime scene tape gave way from the threshold of the door and floated to the floor. His lips curled, and without pause he pushed the door open. When he stepped into the room the chair that was lodged under the knob of the closet door was banging and bumping and rocking. He took a step only to hear the snap and crunch of broken glass beneath his feet. He paused to look down, and that's when the chair wobbled to the left, giving way to fall to the floor. The closet door burst open. Fiona tumbled out, landing on the floor with a grunt.

"Fiona!" He rushed over to help her up.

Holding and shaking her head, Fiona took in a deep breath of air. "Nathan! Sara Holloway killed Alexis, only her name isn't Sara Holloway, its Amber Archer. Silja and I used to dance with her years ago at PBT. The dance teachers didn't like her—" Nathan turned her head to the side while she explained. He was busy examining the blood dried in her strawberry blonde locks. "Amber, or Sara, as she now calls herself, killed Alexis to get the principal dancer position. I can't believe it! How could someone do something so awful just to move ahead? Well, I suppose it goes on all the time in big corporations, but to kill a fellow dancer—a friend, how terrible is that? Are you paying attention?"

"I am. But you need to go to the hospital. I think you might need some stitches. There's glass on the floor. What did she hit you with?"

Wincing, Fiona gingerly touched the back of her head. "There was a vase on the vanity. I'm guessing that you got her?"

Carefully, Nathan lifted her from the floor, set the chair upright, and then eased her onto the chair. "Yes, Sara Holloway AKA Amber Archer is in custody." He pulled out his cell, dialed a few numbers. "Dalton… found Fiona. We need an ambulance. She's not hurt seriously, but she needs medical attention. We're in Alexis Cartwright's dressing room."

Closing her eyes, Fiona breathed in heavily. Thinking that she was fainting, Nathan grabbed her by the shoulders to steady her. He asked, "Are you alright, Fiona? Fiona…"

—ᨁ—

Nathan's voice seemed far away, but then her eyes fluttered open. Favoring him with a svelte smile, Fiona asked, "Do you feel it? I can. Alexis is at peace. She knows that Sara has been caught. She can rest now. She feels free to cross over to the other side."

Nathan glanced around the room and to the ceiling, as if Alexis would appear. He looked back at Fiona, amazed. "You can really feel all that?" She nodded. "I believe you. Can I ask you something?"

"I suppose."

"Are you clairvoyant?"

Fiona slid deeper into the chair. It was a solid question. Was she? She truly never thought about it before this moment. What were the qualities of a clairvoyant? Yes, she had a relationship with her late grandmother, Evelyn Burrell. It was subtle, but it was indeed present. Did that qualify her as a clairvoyant? She hardly believed it to be so. She would have to do some research on the subject when she got home. And then another round of thoughts hit her. If she were clairvoyant, would Nathan look at her differently? Would he think she was some kind of freak? A weirdo? Or worse—not dating material?

"Fiona…"

Her gaze flicked to his, realizing that he'd been trying to get her attention for several seconds.

In a soft coaxing voice, Nathan asked, "Did you make the stairs move at your house?"

"Oh, goodness no!"

"Okay…you wouldn't tell me then, will you tell me now?"

"Um—" Fiona let out a beleaguered indecisive sigh. Just then, Silja appeared at the doorway along with David, Mistress Adele, and a crowd of dancers.

"Fiona!" Silja cried out. "Are you okay? Dalton said you needed medical attention."

Relieved by the interruption, Fiona said, "I'm going to be just fine. Looks like I'll be sitting in the audience after all for the performance. I missed the entire dress rehearsal."

"Nonsense," Mistress Adele said as she pushed to the front of the group. "You're a hero, Fiona. I think all the dancers would agree to an emergency dress rehearsal tomorrow afternoon at one o'clock. If you're up to it."

Fiona looked at Silja's coaxing eyes, and David's cajoling smile. Throwing her hands in the air, she said, "Oh, why not? I don't think anything could stop me at this point."

Mistress Adele clasped her hands to her chest. "Good! We're running out of dancers to play the roles!"

The dancers clapped their hands in agreement.

Fifteen

Bang! Thump! Thump! Bang! Bang! Crash!
Fiona sat straight up in her bed. Harriet wiggled under the blankets until her head peeked out from underneath. She let out a weary bark. The bedroom door opened, and Silja slipped through.

"I think someone is breaking in!" she whispered in a high pitched voice.

"At six-thirty in the morning?" Fiona questioned. "That doesn't seem like prime burglary hours."

Bang! Bang! Slam!

They flinched. Harriet growled from under the blankets.

"It's coming from the basement," Silja supplied. "I'm telling you, someone's coming in through that flimsy door of yours! We should call the police!"

Tossing the blankets aside, Fiona got out of the bed. "Well, they aren't very quiet burglars." She shrugged into her robe. "Before we hit the panic button, I'm going to see what all the racket is about." She padded into the hallway with Silja on her heels. Harriet reluctantly followed along, growling, more out of frustration from being woken up way too early than anything else.

Hesitating at the top of the stairs, they could hear a low murmur of voices coming from the basement. Nostrils wide, Fiona sniffed the air—fresh coffee was brewing. "Hmmm…"

"How can you be so calm? I can hear them talking. They're probably boasting about how easy it was to break in to this house," Silja whispered.

"They must not be too much of a threat. Evelyn's got coffee on. C'mon."

Suddenly realizing they were not going to return to the warm comfy bed, Harriet darted down the stairs, barking more boldly now at the would-be intruders. Fiona and Silja trailed the little bundle of fluff. When they arrived at the basement door, Silja put her hand on Fiona's shoulder. "Are you sure we shouldn't call the police before we barge in on the burglars?"

Fiona pressed her ear to the door. She could hear muffled laughter. "They're either very happy burglars or they're drunk—either way, I'm thinking they're harmless." She opened the door. Harriet darted through her feet and down the old wooden stairs. Fiona turned to Silja wearing a snarky smirk. "She's such a little Rottweiler. I couldn't be more proud." The girls made their way downward until they could see four people standing around the opening where the old basement door once was. The cold February breeze swept through the dank basement space.

Harriet jumped up on Nathan's legs, barking merrily. He turned. "Look who's here! Good morning, Harriet." His gaze met Fiona's. He smiled, and she returned the favor. "Good morning, Ms. Quinn. Hope your head is feeling better."

"It's feeling just fine, thank you, Detective Landry." She tossed him a demure grin. "Sooo, what's this?"

"We felt it was our obligation as your local police force to make sure your basement door was secure." He pointed to an officer who was holding a brand new metal door. "You remember, Wyatt Hays…" Wyatt peeked out from behind the door to nod at the girls. "And of course Officer Dalton felt he should help out as well." Officer Dalton smiled.

"I know who you are," Fiona said when her eyes fell upon a thin blonde woman, who was holding a hammer, standing at Officer Dalton's side. "You're the policewoman who delivered coffee every night to Officer Dalton."

"Tavia Andrews, Dalton's fiancé," Tavia said, extending her hand out to Fiona, who gladly shook it.

Eyebrows raised, Fiona shot Silja an *I told you so* look. Silja rolled her eyes. Pulling her robe tautly around her body, Fiona made her way to the open doorway. "It's so sweet of you to take the time to do this, but you didn't have—"

"We wanted to, Fiona. I didn't want to have to worry about someone breaking into this door again."

"But Nathan—"

"No buts…besides, we've already got the old door out. We can't leave it like this now. Hope we didn't wake you with all the noise."

"No problem. We should be up anyway. We've got that emergency rehearsal this afternoon," Silja said.

"What can I do to help?" Fiona asked.

Grinning, Wyatt poked his head out from behind the door he'd been holding up. "That coffee smells awful good." He poked Nathan in the ribs. "Not like the stuff you make. You could patch a roof with Landry's coffee."

The officers all laughed. Nathan shrugged.

"Coming right up!" Fiona announced, hurrying toward the stairs.

"I'll give you a hand," Nathan said, following.

"I know that Cynthia and Calvin are being arraigned on Monday, but have you heard anything more?" Fiona asked as they climbed the stairs.

"The coroner believes that the crowbar that Calvin intended to use on you was indeed the weapon he used to kill Monroe McCarthy, only he didn't bother or think to wipe it down for prints or blood deposits. Seems Kleppner wasn't nearly as clever as Amber Archer. I spoke with Detective Kearns on the phone. They are reopening the investigation into Samantha

Wells' murder. No surprise there. He'll be in Pittsburgh by Monday afternoon. I've got a gut feeling that when Pittsburgh is done with Ms. Montgomery, she'll be extradited to Seattle to face murder charges there, too."

"Whatta shame."

"It always is, Fiona. It always is."

—◊◊◊—

Even though the afternoon rehearsal went off without a hitch, when the curtain opened for the actual performance of Coppelia, Fiona's stomach was in a knot. Thankfully, as the ballet progressed through the acts, she settled into her role. Friday night's performance seemed like a blur—it went so quickly. Before she knew it she and David were holding hands while taking their final bows and blowing kisses to the audience who appeared to be totally enthralled with them.

After the show Nathan brought a dozen red roses to her. Tossing her a wink, Silja whispered, "Red roses—the color of romance."

"*Silja…*" Fiona scolded.

Saturday's performance came easier and moved along just as swiftly. Fiona tried to hold on to the moments. She felt like Cinderella at the ball. When the curtain fell after the Sunday matinee, her impromptu role as Coppelia would come to a sweeping end. The costumes would disappear. The tiaras would seemingly evaporate. She would be a ballerina no more. It would be time to return to the hum-drum of reality. She would just be ordinary Fiona Quinn—the ordinary kindergarten teacher from Pittsburgh.

Sigh.

She was shocked to find Nathan standing backstage after the show with a bouquet of white roses. "I'm surprised to see you," she said, taking in the flowers' wonderful scent. "You saw the show last night."

"And I loved it. I wanted to see my favorite ballerina dance again tonight," he told her.

Once again, Fiona was feeling the flush on her cheeks and that old familiar flutter in her stomach—it couldn't be nerves. The show was over.

Silja whispered in her ear, "White roses—the color of purity. Yeah, he's into you—big time."

"*Silja*..." She cleared her throat. "I'm a kindergarten teacher, not a nun."

—⁓—

It was inevitable. Sunday afternoon would arrive and so would the final performance of Coppelia. Fiona's heart felt heavy when the curtains came to a close, and yet the overwhelming feeling of pride and accomplishment filled her soul. It was short lived, but whatta come back!

"Ms. Quinn! Ms. Quinn!" several tiny voices called out. Fiona looked up to see three of her students running toward her with pink roses in their hands. Their mothers hung back wearing grins at their children's delight. The little girls' eyes were full of wonderment at the sight of their teacher dressed in a dazzling costume and all the beautiful ballerinas gathered in the backstage area.

"You were wonderful, Ms. Quinn!" one girl told her.

"I wanna be a ballerina just like you when I grow up," another exclaimed, while the third little girl fingered the sequins on her costume.

"Thank you, girls, but I'm not a—"

A warm arm wrapped around her shoulder. "She's a fantastic ballerina, isn't she, girls?" Nathan said, as he handed her a bouquet of pink roses. Fiona's lips curled in delight.

Hmmm, she found herself thinking, *wonder what this color means.*

Fiona looked around for Silja. She had always been right there to enlighten her with such information. She searched through the crowd to see a handsome, broad shouldered man dressed in a smart Armani suit stroll toward Silja with an armful of red roses and a pride-filled curl to his lips. Silja threw her arms around him. Their lips met.

"Whoa," Nathan said. "Who's that?"

Fiona smiled. "I have no doubt that's Silja's husband, Grant. I'll bet she's happy to see him."

"Sure looks like it from here." He turned her toward him. "So, is my favorite ballerina slash super sleuth slash most adorable kindergarten teacher I've ever met, available for dinner sometime soon?"

Shaking her head, she laughed. "Like how soon?"

"Like tonight?"

Fiona couldn't have suppressed the ear to ear grin on her face if her very life depended on it. "I'd love that."

Nathan reached in his pocket, smiled, and then pulled out a tiny square of foil. "Snickers?"

END

COMING SOON FROM FIONA QUINN

Thank you for reading *Murder on Pointe*. Join Fiona and the gang for a Christmas whodunit in her next mystery, *Merry Murder*, coming in November 2016. Don't miss it!

For more information on the *Fiona Quinn Mystery Series* and C.S. McDonald's children's books, please visit her website:

www.csmcdonaldbooks.com

BRAND NEW FROM GEORGE'S BARN…

GEORGE TURNS **GREEN**!

About C.S. McDonald

For twenty-six years C.S. McDonald's life whirled around a song and a dance. She was a professional dancer and choreographer. During that time she choreographed many musicals and an opera for the Pittsburgh Savoyards. In 2011 she retired from her dance career to write. Under her real name, Cindy McDonald, she writes murder-suspense and romantic suspense novels. In 2014 she added the pen name, C.S. McDonald, to write children's books for her grandchildren. Now she adds the Fiona Quinn Mysteries to that expansion.

She decided to write the cozy mystery series for her young granddaughters.

Ms. McDonald resides on her Thoroughbred farm known as Fly by Night Stables near Pittsburgh, Pennsylvania with her husband, Bill, and her Cocker Spaniel, Allister.

You can learn more about C.S. McDonald and her books here: www.csmcdonaldbooks.com

Made in the USA
Columbia, SC
01 October 2018